She hadn't b
had met Dani

He hesitated in the doorway, a dream in the shadows, then strolled into the glow of the overhead lights, her knight who had come to carry her away to happily-ever-after. His navy slacks and yellow pullover shirt were both pretty much a mess, and he hadn't even combed his hair. But he was the most beautiful sight she had ever seen.

He stopped a few feet inside the door. "Hi," he said, dazzling her with a sheepish grin.

If she didn't know better, she'd say he sounded shy. "Hi, yourself."

"My name's Daniel. What's yours?"

A silent message passed between them. The promise of a new beginning was sealed. Anticipation and excitement danced across her skin. "Sara. My name is Sara."

GINA FIELDS is a lifelong native of northeast Georgia. She is married to Terry and they have two very active, young sons. When Gina is not writing, singing, or playing piano, or doing one of a hundred homemaking activities, she enjoys volunteering for Special Olympics.

Books by Gina Fields

Familiar Strangers

Gina Fields

Heartsong Presents

To "Ma" and "Pa"—Thanks for accepting me as one of your own and for giving me such a wonderful husband.

A note from the author:
I love to hear from my readers! You may correspond with me by writing:
                          Gina Fields
                          Author Relations
                          PO Box 719
                          Uhrichsville, OH 44683

ISBN 1-57748-981-0

FAMILIAR STRANGERS

All of the characters and events in this book are fictitious. Any resemblance to actual persons, living or dead, or to actual events is purely coincidental.

Cover illustration by Chris Cocozza.

PRINTED IN THE U.S.A.

one

"Mama, are you going to marry Jeff?"

Sara Jennings tucked the pillow-soft comforter around her daughter's small body. "I don't know. Maybe someday."

Chloe promptly wormed her arms from beneath the binding cover. Like her mother, she didn't like feeling confined.

. "That's what you always say," the four year old said.

Sara eased down to sit on the edge of the bed. "I know it is, but I haven't made my mind up yet." She scooped up a one-eyed giraffe from the foot of the bed and nestled the tired-looking toy into her daughter's waiting arms. *Poor George,* Sara thought. She really should find a button and replace his missing eye.

"But if you marry Jeff," Chloe persisted, "then I would have a daddy, like Missy and April."

Sara sighed. How did one explain to a child so young why she didn't have a daddy when her two best friends from her Sunday school class did? The same way she always did, Sara decided, wondering how much longer she could get away with the same answer.

"Sweetie, do you remember what I told you the other day about some boys and girls having two parents and some having only one?"

Chloe gave a doleful nod.

"It doesn't mean you're any less special than the children who have both a mommy and a daddy. It just means I get to love you twice as much."

Chloe dropped her gaze to the spiked hair atop the giraffe's head. "I know," she responded in an I've-heard-it-all-before tone. "But I still want a daddy."

5

Sara's shoulders rose and fell in dejection. Ever since Jeff Chandler, the widowed director of a Chicago homeless shelter, had asked Sara to marry him six weeks ago, she and Chloe had had this same conversation several times over. And Chloe's answer was always the same. *"I want a daddy."* Not *"I want Jeff to be my daddy."*

Chloe's vague answer left Sara wondering if Chloe wanted Jeff, in particular, for a father or if she simply wanted *"a daddy."*

Since the marriage proposal, Sara had watched closely for signs of a developing parent-child relationship between Jeff and Chloe, but so far she'd seen little evidence of any. Sure, Jeff and Chloe were close, in an uncle-niece sort of way. But that special bond, like Jeff shared with his own two adolescent children, simply wasn't there.

And that alone gave Sara pause in making her decision.

If and when she ever decided to marry, the prospective husband would have to acknowledge and accept he was getting a package deal—a wife and daughter. Sara would rather die an old maid than have Chloe feel inferior to stepsiblings. Or anyone else, for that matter.

Sara leaned over, and Chloe rubbed noses with her mother. "Good night. Sleep tight," Sara chimed. "And don't let the bed bugs bite!" they finished together.

Giggling, Chloe reached up and rewarded her mother with a hug and a butterfly kiss on the cheek. Then, turning to her side, she snuggled George the Giraffe to her chest and closed her eyes.

Sara reached over to turn off the yard-sale lamp that sat on the nightstand she had borrowed from her landlady, but then she paused to study her daughter. Chloe's long, tawny lashes curled against rosy cheeks, and her hair had grown so that it flowed like silk around her shoulders. Hard to believe they'd already celebrated her fourth birthday. Where was the baby that had nuzzled at her breast, cuddled on her shoulder, offered her toothless grins? Where had the last four years gone?

Into one mindless day after another, Sara silently answered her own question. A cycle of perpetual routine she had come to accept as her destiny.

And today had been no different.

She had gotten up at six A.M., showered and dressed for work, and had breakfast with Chloe and Evelyn Porter, the regal, elderly lady from whom Sara rented two rooms. Then Sara had bundled up Chloe in a thick sweater and warm toboggan—because, even in late May, Illinois mornings could be brisk—and together they had walked to one of the four houses Sara cleaned weekly in the upscale Chicago sub-urb where they lived.

While Sara scrubbed toilets, dusted furniture, and battled cobwebs, Chloe, as usual, had been content watching one of her favorite cartoon videos or playing with one of the games Sara brought along. But as always, guilt had pricked Sara's conscience at least twice that day because her daughter spent so much time entertaining herself.

As a single mom, Sara found meager comfort knowing she was doing the best she could do. After all, any plans she had made, any goals she had set for herself, had been ripped from her grasp five years ago. Now her plans and goals all centered on Chloe.

When Sara had finished her household tasks, she and Chloe walked back to Mrs. Porter's, where Sara helped her landlady prepare supper. Then, after the three shared the evening meal and the kitchen was put back in order, had come Sara's favorite time of day, when she tucked Chloe into bed with a hug and a prayer.

Another ordinary day. A day like any other. Nothing grand or spectacular about it.

In fact, Sara knew of only one truly grand and spectacular day since she'd come to live with Mrs. Porter almost five years ago. That was the day Chloe had been born. That day, that hour, that single moment had marked a new beginning for Sara. The instant she looked into her daughter's eyes, she knew God was giving her a second chance at life. She could either take it or throw it back in His face and continue mourning the life she had lost.

Sara had decided to take it.

And now, looking down at her daughter's face, she didn't have one single shred of regret. Reaching over, she brushed a strand of hair from Chloe's cheek and she was reminded, not for the first time, how different she and her daughter were. Chloe had straight blond hair and huge sapphire-blue eyes, while Sara had corkscrew curly brown hair and light brown eyes. Except for their slight frames, Sara couldn't find a single physical similarity between her and her child.

Did Chloe favor her father? Only God knew.

Pulling the comforter up a few more inches on Chloe's shoulders, Sara shook off the melancholy spirit stealing over her. She would not waste time feeling sorry for herself; she had too much to be thankful for: a man who loved her enough to want to spend the rest of his life with her; a friend in Evelyn Porter, who had offered Sara a home when she was homeless; and a perfectly healthy daughter who gave her a reason to face one tedious day after another. A surge of love rose in Sara's chest and almost overflowed in the form of tears. All things considered, she was pretty well blessed.

She leaned down and planted a soft kiss on her daughter's cheek. Chloe's eyes fluttered open, then slowly drifted down again as the child slipped from twilight sleep into dreamland. Sara switched off the lamp and crept from the room.

Stifling a yawn, she went down the red-carpeted steps leading to the first floor. There was still plenty she needed to do: fold the laundry, unload the dishwasher. But those things could wait until morning. This had been a long day, and Mrs. Porter's chamomile tea smelled too delicious. All Sara wanted to do was pour herself a cup of the pungent brew and curl up with the suspense novel her landlady had brought home from the library that day.

Massaging her nape, Sara padded in socked feet across the marble foyer floor into a kitchen dimly lit by a single twenty-five-watt bulb that glowed from the range hood. Sara smiled as she ambled to the stove. Mrs. Porter might be "financially secure," as the refined lady so modestly put it, but when it came to cutting monetary corners, she was downright miserly.

Sara, on the other hand, was frugal because she had to be. She reached into the cabinet for a cup and saucer. Someday, when she saved enough money to buy herself and Chloe a home of their own, light would be an item on which she would not scrimp. Not only on the inside of the house, but on the outside as well. Abundant sunlight and wide-open spaces. One day, she and Chloe would have both—if Sara had to scrub a dozen toilets a day to get them.

"Sara?"

She was stirring a teaspoon of honey into her tea when Mrs. Porter's genteel, high-pitched voice filtered into the kitchen from the adjoining room.

"I'll be right there." Sara put her spoon in the sink.

"You may want to hurry!"

Frowning, Sara glanced over her shoulder at the open doorway leading to the adjoining family room. Were her ears deceiving her or was that a note of urgency she'd heard in Mrs. Porter's voice?

"Please," Mrs. Porter added in what sounded like an afterthought, as though she'd suddenly realized she had stepped out of character by using a tone other than her usually calm and proper one.

Gingerly balancing her cup on her saucer, Sara headed for the door.

Her landlady sat in a plush recliner, her eyes riveted on the television screen. The glow from a nearby floor lamp's low-wattage bulb reflected off her short white hair like a silver halo.

"Is something wrong, Mrs. Porter?" Sara asked.

Her gaze fixed on the screen, Mrs. Porter said, "I think you'll want to see this."

When Sara glanced toward the TV, she thought she knew why Mrs. Porter had called to her. On the screen was one of the most peaceful coastal scenes Sara had ever seen. Foamy waves lapped lazily over cream-colored sand, then slipped quietly, almost reluctantly, it seemed, back out to sea. Vigilant seagulls sailed over the water, and restless palm leaves danced in the wind.

Mrs. Porter knew Sara loved the ocean, knew she dreamed of seeing it one day for herself. Every time she saw a picture of the rocky cliffs bordering the Pacific or read about the mysteries of the blue Atlantic, longing filled her heart. But only in her imagination could she walk the endless stretches of beach, revel in cool water tugging at her ankles, lift her face to the wind's salty kiss.

Her shoulders rose and fell as a wistful sigh escaped her chest. *Someday,* she told herself. *Someday. . .*

A suave-looking gentleman appeared on the screen. The wind kicked up the front of his well-groomed gray hair as he strolled up the beach. "We come to you tonight from the tranquil beaches of Quinn Island, South Carolina," he said. "A place where southern hospitality is in abundant supply, and residents of this small, close-knit community pride themselves on maintaining one of the lowest crime rates in the Southeast."

He stopped and squared off to face the camera. "But almost five years ago, on the night of August eighth, tragedy struck Quinn Island with as much force as the battering winds of a class five hurricane, when one of their own, Lydia Anne Quinn, disappeared *without a trace.*" The face of an attractive young woman, smiling like she held the world by its reins, flashed on the screen.

Sara stared at the screen for a moment in stunned silence. Then she blinked, and her world tilted, teetered on its side for a few precarious seconds, then tumbled from its axis, sending her stomach into a wild tailspin. She felt the blood drain from her face, and the cup and saucer slipped from her limp fingers. She was vaguely aware of searing liquid scalding her denim-clad right knee and seeping through the wool of her socks.

This can't be happening, she told herself, thinking any second now she'd wake up. When a sharp edge of broken china penetrated her sock and bit into her heel, she realized she was not dreaming. The day she had both longed for and feared had finally arrived. And life as she knew it was about to change. *Forever.*

Because the face on the TV screen. . .was hers.

&

Still strong and agile at seventy-two, Mrs. Porter had helped Sara to the sofa before the younger woman completely collapsed, then fetched a Band-Aid for Sara's bleeding heel. The two women now sat side by side, holding hands, as they watched bits and pieces of Sara's life—the one she'd lived before waking up in a Chicago hospital five years ago.

Once Sara had watched every missing-person show televised in the Chicago area, thinking maybe, just maybe, a story would evolve that would lead to her identity. Even if she didn't have a family looking for her, she figured, surely *someone* would have noticed her absence—a boss, a coworker, a friend.

But, after a while, when episode after episode passed without revealing anything that might be of consequence to her past life, she grew weary of the waiting, the anticipation, and then the letdown. So she'd stopped watching, stopped waiting for someone to find her, and she accepted that whoever might have known her in her past life had either given up searching—or hadn't cared enough to ever begin to search. Now, here she was, on national TV. Someone *had* cared enough. Enough that they had never given up looking for her.

Aside from the throbbing of her now-bandaged heel, she was too shocked to feel anything but numb.

"Lydia Anne Quinn led a charmed and privileged life," came the skilled voice of the screen host. "She was born twenty-nine years ago on April second, the oldest daughter of William Quinn, the partner in a successful charter fishing business, and his wife, Margaret Quinn, a former teacher who left the classroom to become a full-time mom after Lydia was born."

"I'm twenty-nine years old," Sara whispered in awe. Her doctor had estimated her age, and every year Mrs. Porter insisted Sara celebrate her birthday with Chloe. Just last month, Sara had celebrated her twenty-seventh.

But she wasn't twenty-seven—she was twenty-nine. And her birthday wasn't April twenty-sixth, like Chloe's—it was April second.

After five years in ageless limbo, she finally had a beginning.

A portrait of herself and three other people, obviously her family, flashed on the screen. Her father appeared to be only a couple inches taller than her mother. He had the same curly brown hair and light brown eyes as Sara. Her sister, a tall, willowy blond, favored her mother.

Sara studied the portrait intently to see if something in one of the faces would kindle a spark of recognition, a sense of connection. But she felt nothing. They were all total strangers to her.

"Lydia was a high achiever," the host continued. "A straight-A student, head cheerleader, and homecoming queen her senior year in high school. She graduated summa cum laude from South Carolina State University. At the time of her disappearance, she owned and operated Lydia's Boutique, a prosperous dress shop located on Quinn Island's mainland. And she was planning to marry this man"—the scene changed to a handsome young man—"Attorney Daniel

Matthews, who was the last person known to have talked to Lydia the night of her disappearance."

Sara's breath caught in her throat. She had been engaged. . . to an attorney. . .and he was *beautiful*. He wore his dark brown hair cut short on the sides, a little longer on top, and combed back in a side part—with the exception of one rakish lock that dipped toward his right brow. His wedge-shaped jaw, olive complexion, and prominent cheekbones hinted at an ancestry other than pure Anglo. Native American, maybe? His brown eyes held a touch of sadness that made Sara's pounding heart roll over.

"Lydia was on her way home from New York," the young attorney explained to the off-camera interviewer. "She'd driven up three days before to attend some fashion shows and order new designs for her dress shop. Normally, she would have flown, but she'd just purchased a new car the week before and wanted to drive it."

His educated southern drawl had a smooth, velvet-edged quality that captivated Sara. Without thought, she pulled her hands free from Mrs. Porter's and leaned forward a couple of inches, her own hands clasped tightly in her lap. Daniel Matthews was seated, she noticed, on a sofa in someone's living room. Whose home was he in? His? Hers? Her parents'?

"Her mother usually took these trips with her," he went on, "but Mrs. Quinn had undergone hip surgery a few days before, and she wasn't able to go along. Her sister Jennifer stayed behind to run the shop. So this was a solo trip for Lydia. Her first."

An indefinable emotion clouded his features. He paused, dropping his gaze to some point below the camera lens. Seconds hung in suspension while he appeared to struggle with his private thoughts. Then he raised his head and lifted his shoulders a few inches, as though summoning the fortitude to plow ahead. "Before she left, I bought her a cellular phone so she could check in with her parents or me while she was on the road, or call someone if her car broke down.

"The night she was expected home, she phoned me around eleven o'clock. She had crossed the South Carolina state line, but she had run into a traffic jam. She said she was going to get off the expressway somewhere above Darlington and try to work her way around it.

"I knew some of those rural roads could be deserted, especially so late at night, so I tried to talk her into staying on the interstate. But she told me not to worry, that she had a map."

He closed his eyes, and a raw grief flickered across his face. He swallowed hard, then wet his lips. Somehow, Sara sensed he was steeling himself against his next words.

Finally, he opened haunted eyes. "The last words she said to me were, 'I'll call you when I get home. I love you. Goodbye.' " His voice, as he delivered his final statement, was raspy with emotion.

Sara took a deep shuddery breath and pressed a trembling hand to her chest. Unexpected tears warmed her eyes. This man had loved her. Deeply. She could see it in his grieving expression, hear it in his tortured voice. And she had loved him, had told him so just before something dark and horrible had taken away what might have been a precious memory.

The scene switched to a foreign-made sports car sitting alongside a dark, deserted stretch of highway. The driver's door stood open. The host stepped into view on the right side of the screen.

"But Lydia didn't make it home that night," he said. "Instead, Daniel answered a knock on his door three hours later to find the Quinn Island sheriff and a deputy standing on his doorstep. The news they had to deliver was not good. They had received a call from the Darlington Police Department. Lydia's car had been found, abandoned, alongside a sparsely populated stretch of highway outside the Darlington city limits."

As the host spoke, a patrol car pulled up and stopped behind the sports coupe. Two actors portraying police officers got out and approached the abandoned vehicle cautiously. They continued playing their role while the host resumed the story.

"The driver's door was standing open, and Lydia's purse and cellular phone were found on the front passenger seat. Next to the flat rear tire on the passenger's side, a crowbar with traces of hair and blood was found."

Sara's hand rose and touched the jagged scar on her left temple, the one doctors had said probably robbed her of her memory. Had the crowbar delivered the blow? What about the four-inch laceration on the back of her head and the one over her right ear, the bruises and broken bones. . .?

Like hot water breaking into a boil, anger exploded in Sara's chest. The crowbar had not delivered the damaging blows to her defenseless body, the hands that held it had.

The doctors had told her she'd been brought into the hospital in the wee hours of August twelfth. According to the story unfolding on the TV screen, that had been a little more than two days after her disappearance. For forty-eight hours she must have been in the hands of her assailants. During that time, she had been stripped of all she was, all she had been, all she had loved.

A raw ache rose in her throat. Closing her eyes, she wrapped her arms around her waist and bit down hard on her lower lip. Faceless demons still haunted her. Demons that had robbed her of her memory, her past. The results of their actions, however, had left an irrevocable mark upon her life.

She squeezed her eyes shut tighter and started rocking, trying to shut out the harsh reality that wrapped around her like a fog. She had a family who loved her. . .and a fiancé who was still searching for her.

After almost five years of struggling to put some sort of life together for herself and her daughter, she had been found. She knew with certainty she was going home, but she also knew that things would never be as they once were. Not for her. Not for her family. Not for a man named Daniel

Matthews. Because she was not the same woman who had left them half a decade ago. A sob tore from her throat. Could her parents, her sister, her fiancé accept the woman she had become—and the horrible things that had happened to her?

She felt Mrs. Porter's arms slip around her shoulders, and she turned her face into the crook of the older woman's neck. She was going home to a place she knew nothing about, a family of strangers, and a man she had promised to marry. What kind of homecoming would it be?

And what would they think about Chloe?

two

At a television station in Manhattan, Daniel Matthews stood in the *Without a Trace* studio room, his gaze on a big-screen television boxed inside a pewter-gray wall. Arms crossed and feet braced shoulders' width apart, he watched as the story of his fiancée's disappearance unfolded. Behind him, eight telephone operators, stationed in two rows of four each, sat at individual computer terminals, headsets in place, waiting for the first call to come in.

Odd, Daniel thought as Lydia's picture gave way to a portrait of her and her family, *how losing someone you love can make time stand still.* He still looked for her face in every crowd and around every corner. Still surfed the net for countless hours in hopes of finding a clue to what had happened to her. Still waited each night for the phone to ring, for her to tell him she had made it home safely after all. At least once each day, he relived that fateful night when she'd been abducted from her car on a deserted stretch of highway north of Darlington.

He scrubbed a weary hand down his face, his mind buzzing through the brutal days that had followed. After six months of relentless searching proved futile, the sheriff had tried to convince Daniel the worst had happened. That Lydia had been killed and whatever was left of her would probably never be found. But Daniel refused to believe that. Only when a body was discovered and positively identified would he accept that she was gone from him forever.

"How're you holding up?"

Daniel looked to his right, wondering how long Bob Siler, the head producer of *Without a Trace,* had been standing next

17

to him. "I'm okay," Daniel answered, massaging the back of his neck.

"Really? You don't look okay."

A grin pulled at one corner of Daniel's mouth. He knew Bob's words were spoken out of concern and not criticism. Their frequent communications over the last few months had led to an amicable friendship.

"It's just the anticipation," Daniel said. "You'd think after five years I'd be used to it."

But he wasn't, and he doubted he ever would be. Every time a clue trickled in, hinting at what might have happened to Lydia, his reaction was always the same. Sweaty palms, a stiff neck, and a heart that pounded so hard his ears burned.

Then would come the letdown, a gut-wrenching twist to his insides that left his chest feeling hollow when the clue led to another dead-end.

"Daniel, you know what the chances are," Bob said as though reading Daniel's mind.

"Yeah, I know," Daniel replied. *Slim to none.* That's what everyone, including Bob, had told Daniel. In fact, from the start, Bob had been so negative about a program segment on Lydia's abduction, Daniel had been shocked when the producer had called two months ago to tell him the network had decided to air the story.

Of course, six months' worth of weekly calls from Daniel to the station might have had something to do with the decision. The show's producers had eventually figured out the persistent attorney wasn't going to give up until the story of his fiancée's disappearance was told. Since all else had failed, Daniel figured getting her picture on national TV was his best chance of finding her—maybe his last chance.

"I just want you to be prepared," Bob said.

Daniel chose not to respond. How did one prepare himself for the unknown? He jammed his fists into his pockets to keep from drying his damp palms on his dark dress slacks. "How long does it usually take before the calls start coming in?"

"It varies. Sometimes immediately. Sometimes a couple of hours. We've even had a few come in several days after a program aired."

A picture of Lydia's dress shop flashed on the screen, and a painful knot rose in Daniel's throat. The wedding gown she'd planned to wear less than a month after the date of her disappearance still hung in the back of that shop. Would he ever see her march down the aisle in it?

A buzzer indicated an incoming call. Pinpricks of anticipation raced up the back of Daniel's neck. Both men turned, but only Bob hurried to the operator who had answered the call. Daniel stood waiting, praying, his head throbbing from a sudden rush of blood.

Then Bob looked Daniel's way and motioned him over. Daniel sprinted across the room to join Bob, who was huddled over the operator as she transferred information onto the computer.

"What did you say your name was, ma'am?" the operator asked, then typed in *Elizabeth Bradford*.

"And you're calling from where?"

Riverbend, Illinois.

"I know that area," Bob mused. "It's a ritzy suburb north of Chicago."

Ritzy, Daniel repeated to himself. Lydia would like ritzy. He held his breath.

"You said Ms. Quinn looks like someone you know?" the operator continued.

Yes.

Daniel clenched a fist, ready to punch the air with glee.

She looks like Sara Jennings, my cleaning lady.

Daniel's mounting hopes dissipated like a warm vapor in a cold wind. The last thing Lydia would be was a cleaning lady. She hated housework. In fact, before her disappearance, she had paid someone else to clean her one-bedroom apartment once a week to keep from having to do it herself.

The sudden drop from elation to disappointment left Daniel shaky. He ran trembling fingers through his hair.

Bob glanced back over his shoulder. "You don't think it's worth following up?"

Daniel released his pent-up breath with force. "No. The last thing you'd find Lydia doing for a living is cleaning houses."

"Anything's possible," Bob said. "I think we should at least look into it."

"Sure." Daniel hunched his shoulders. "Why not? Like you said, 'Anything's possible.' "

But Lydia? A cleaning lady? He didn't think so.

Spirits weighed down, he lumbered back across the room and resumed his vigil in front of the large-screen television and waited for the next call to come in.

❧

Daniel closed the lid on his suitcase. Last night, he'd waited at the studio for two hours after the show ended. Aside from the strange call from the lady in Riverbend, Illinois, there had been no other calls. Bob had told him not to lose hope so soon, but the sympathy in the producer's eyes had belied his true thoughts. *Lydia's gone,* his expression had said. *Time to move on.*

Daniel ran a weary hand over his face. Maybe Bob was right. Maybe it was time to move on. Daniel just didn't know how without Lydia.

A knock sounded on his motel room door. He opened it to find the bellhop, standing at attention, his uniform as fresh and crisp as a navy captain's.

"Your cab is ready, sir."

"Thank you." Daniel turned to retrieve his suitcase.

"I'll get that, sir." In the blink of an eye, the bellhop slipped past Daniel and claimed the luggage.

Unaccustomed to being waited on, Daniel checked various

pockets for his keys, wallet, and plane ticket to keep from cracking his knuckles, a nervous habit he'd picked up shortly after Lydia's disappearance. Before stepping outside into the hallway, he slung his navy blazer over his shoulder and turned one last time to scan the opulent suite the *Without a Trace* network had provided for him. Lydia would have loved the room. The blue velvet window dressings, the mottled marble fireplace, the plush white carpet. She was a woman at home in elegance.

In his mind's eye he saw her pirouetting in delight around the room like a gypsy, a long red dress swirling around her slim ankles and her shiny highlighted hair flowing about her pale shoulders. When she was in a good mood, her laughter and energy were contagious.

"Did I forget something, sir?"

Reluctantly, Daniel turned his attention back to the bellhop standing a few feet down the hall. "No. I was just double-checking, but I think we got everything."

When he looked back into the room, his dancing gypsy was gone.

He pulled a deep breath into his tightening chest, then slowly released a long sigh. "Good-bye, my love," he whispered.

As he closed the door, an eerie sense of finality swept through him. And as he walked away, the words *Move on, Daniel. Time to move on,* seemed to follow him down the hall.

He pressed a generous tip into the bellhop's hand and slid into the car. "Kennedy Airport," he told the cabby. The driver eased his car out into the noisy New York traffic.

They had barely traveled a mile when Daniel's cell phone rang. He dug it out of his blazer pocket and flipped it open. "Hello?"

Silence filled his ear.

"Hello?" he repeated after five seconds.

Silence still, but he thought he heard someone breathing on the other end of the line.

"This is Daniel Matthews. May I help you?"

The line went dead.

Frowning, he pulled the phone away from his ear and pressed the caller ID button. He didn't recognize the number, but the area code triggered something in his memory. After a moment of thought, he realized it was the same area code as the woman who had called the studio the night before. But Daniel wasn't sure about the rest of the number. Could it be the same woman? If so, why was she calling him and not the TV station? And how did she get his number?

Only one way to find out. He hit the button that dialed the number on the display screen.

"Hello." The voice sounded like that of an elderly woman.

"Hello," he returned. "This is Daniel Matthews."

"Yes, Mr. Matthews," came a cheerful reply. "My name is Evelyn Porter. It's so good to finally speak to you."

"Thank you," he said, totally confused. "How did you get this number?"

"Directory assistance."

"Of course," he said, remembering he was having his home calls forwarded to his cellular phone. "What can I do for you?"

"Nothing, really."

Daniel clenched his teeth. Was this someone's idea of a joke? If so, he was in no mood. Tempering the rising anger in his voice, he said, "Then why did you call?"

"I didn't."

"Then who did?"

"The young lady who lives with me."

"And that would be. . .?"

A slight pause, then, "Why don't I just let you talk to her."

Daniel waited while a muffled, inaudible conversation took place on the other end, then a faint click sparked a distant but distinct memory.

An earring. Lydia's earring always clicked on the receiver

when she answered the phone. He sat up straighter in the seat.

"Hello?"

His lungs shut down and his heart slammed against his chest. The voice was hers.

"Hello," she repeated a little louder. "Is. . .anyone there?"

"Lydia? Is that you?"

"I. . .think so."

I think so? What kind of answer was that?

The pressure against his ribs reminded him he wasn't breathing. Slowly, he exhaled. "I don't understand."

"It's a bit complicated, Mr. Matthews. I'd rather not get into it over the phone."

Conflicting emotions tumbled through him. She'd called him *Mr. Matthews*. So formal. So impersonal. Was this another false alarm? Someone looking for a generous handout or public attention? He'd had enough of those in the past five years to last a dozen lifetimes.

"Mr. Matthews?"

But the voice. It was a bit timid and cautious sounding for Lydia, and the southern accent had a slight northern clip. But the sweet-as-honey intonation and the soft-as-silk inflection were definitely hers.

"Are you still there, Mr. Matthews?"

"Yes. Yes, I'm still here. I'm just. . .a little confused." *Make that a lot confused,* he added to himself.

"I'm sorry. I guess I do need to explain a little."

"Please."

He heard a slow, steady intake of breath. "Almost five years ago, sixteen days after Lydia Quinn's disappearance, I woke up in a Chicago hospital. I had been in a coma at least two weeks."

"Why? What happened?"

"I don't know. . .exactly. I couldn't remember." At least four seconds drifted by. "I still can't."

"*Still* can't?"

"That's right."

Daniel searched his mind and came up with only one possible answer. "Amnesia?"

"Yes."

His eyes slid shut. That explained everything. Why she hadn't come home. Why she hadn't called. She hadn't known *where* to come or *who* to call.

Opening his eyes, he pulled a pen from his shirt pocket and his plane ticket from the inside pouch of his blazer. "How do I get there?"

"Before I tell you, Mr. Matthews—"

"Daniel, please," he said with a grimace. If he didn't know better, he'd think he was talking to a stranger. He paused in the midst of balancing the plane ticket on his knee as reality sank in. They *were* strangers. At least he was to her. Right now, she didn't know him from anyone else she might pass on the street. How long before she regained her memory? *Would* she ever regain her memory?

"Okay. Daniel." Her wary voice interrupted his disturbing thoughts. "I think you and I should meet first and make absolutely certain I am Lydia before we get anyone's hopes up."

Get anyone's hopes up? She had to be kidding. His were already flying way above reach. But she had the right idea. Why get her parents' and sister's hopes up until he was absolutely certain she was Lydia? And when he saw her, he would be.

"I agree," he said.

"And would you please not notify *Without a Trace* yet?"

Her request struck him as odd. She had never been one to shun attention. She would have wanted the whole world to know she'd been found. But now was not the time to ponder her reasons for wanting secrecy. He'd agree to anything to get her to tell him where she was. "Okay. If that's what you want."

"It is."

He trapped the ticket between his knee and the heel of his

hand, ready to write down her address.

"I have my reasons," she added, as though she owed him some sort of explanation.

A chilly finger of foreboding slid up Daniel's spine. What had happened to her in the last five years? What had she done with herself? What kind of life had she led?

"This is where I live," came the mysterious yet oh-so-familiar voice.

Daniel snapped to attention and started writing down the information.

෨

Sara hung up the phone softly. She couldn't believe it. She had actually talked to someone from her past. Last night, after the show had ended, she had phoned directory assistance and gotten Daniel Matthews's telephone number, but she had waited until the morning to call. She'd needed time to think, time to figure out the terms on which she would meet him. After all, she had more to think about than herself. She had Chloe.

"Well," Mrs. Porter said from where she sat beside Sara on the family room sofa, "when do we get to meet Mr. Matthews?"

"Soon, I imagine. He's on his way to Kennedy Airport right now. He was in New York for the premier show last night and was on his way to catch his flight back to Quinn Island this morning. But now he's changing his plans. He's going to take the first flight he can get to Chicago. He could be here as early as this afternoon."

Rising, Sara crossed her arms and wandered to the tall window beside the stone fireplace. Sweeping aside the sheers that hung beneath tapered blue damask draperies, she looked out at the small oasis of flowers she had created. The miniature roses climbing a cast-iron fence were just beginning to burst open in brilliant shades of pink. The red azaleas lining the edge of the yard were in full bloom, and the blossoming impatiens in the small flower bed surrounding a cedar bird feeder nodded lazily in the crisp morning breeze.

In her other life had she loved the feel of the earth sifting through her hands? Had she found one of the most amazing things in the world planting a seed and watching it grow?

Had she believed in God?

Does Daniel?

So many questions to be answered. So much territory to be rediscovered. Sara had always thought if this moment ever came, she'd be ready. Now that it had, she wasn't so sure.

Mrs. Porter touched Sara's shoulder. Sara turned to face the closest thing to a family she and her daughter knew. With wise eyes full of understanding, the older woman clasped Sara's hands. "Sara, dear, I know you're scared. But, remember, God sees the big picture. This will all unfold according to His plan."

"I know," Sara said past the mixed emotions that clogged her throat. God had brought her through too much over the past five years for her not to realize He had a hand in her being found. She squeezed Mrs. Porter's soft hands. "It's going to be hard leaving you."

Mrs. Porter's eyes grew misty. "I know. But you'll soon meet a man who loves you so much he's never stopped searching for you. You have a family who's grieved for you for almost five years. Just think of the joy you'll bring them all when you return to them. And you know I'll always be here for you and Chloe, no matter what. I hope you'll remember that."

Sara's own eyes teared. "You can count on it."

The two women embraced in a hug that Sara knew marked the ending of one era of her life and the beginning of another. This heartfelt gesture was a symbol of time shared, joy experienced, and blessing, both great and small, they had brought to one another. The next would be to say good-bye.

three

"Here we are," Daniel told the Chicago taxi driver.

The cabbie shot him an "I-think-I-know-where-I'm-going" look in the rearview mirror as he turned into the entrance of Twin Oaks Subdivision in Riverbend, Chicago.

Unperturbed by the driver's obvious irritation, Daniel grasped the back of the front passenger seat and slid forward, reading the house numbers. After his phone conversation with Lydia that morning, he had managed to secure a flight to Chicago almost immediately. Now, here he was, four hours later, on the brink of a long-awaited reunion with her.

The empty years of searching were almost over.

He craned his neck to read a number partially hidden by a tall flowering bush. Nothing about the affluent neighborhood surprised him. Class suited Lydia, and everything about the stately homes lining the well-kept street bespoke class. He was sure she had fit in well here.

"There it is," he said, pointing to the third house up the street. "Fourteen-oh-one."

The driver swerved up to the curb in front of the colonial-style brick home. Passing the cabbie a generous bill, Daniel said, "Keep the change," and vaulted from the car, hauling his overnight bag behind him.

He strode up the sidewalk and hurdled the two steps leading to the front stoop in one smooth motion. Without pause, he rang the doorbell. Impatiently, he straightened his blazer and finger-combed his hair. When the doorknob rattled, every muscle in his body tensed.

But the woman who opened the door wasn't Lydia. She was an elderly lady with a short crop of silvery-white hair, immaculately applied makeup, and an out-of-style but elegant dark green polyester dress. Pearl-studded earrings as big around as quarters hung from her earlobes, and a generous row of pearls circled her aged neck.

He raised his brows. "Mrs. Porter?"

As she inclined her regal head, a welcoming smile brought a youthful sparkle to her light blue eyes. "So nice to meet you, Mr. Matthews." Her gaze swept down his body and back up again, making him feel like a ten-year-old under wash-up inspection before Sunday dinner.

When her eyes once again met his, one appraising brow inched up her forehead. "I must say, the television cameras didn't do you justice."

Daniel appreciated the woman's attempt at friendly banter, but at the moment he didn't want to waste precious minutes on idle small talk. "Thank you. Is Lydia here?"

"Yes. She's upstairs." Mrs. Porter stepped back, and Daniel entered the foyer. A crystal chandelier hung from a high ceiling, and the walls were dressed in burnished gold wallpaper. The mottled marble floor and the stairway's heavy wooden railing were polished to a glossy sheen. The faint scent of lemon oil and potpourri hung in the air. Obviously someone, perhaps the maid, had recently been cleaning.

Mrs. Porter closed the door and stepped around him. "I'll show you to the living room," she said, then led him toward double doors at the end of the foyer. Glancing back over her shoulder, she added, "Better known in my day as the courting parlor," and sent him a saucy wink.

Daniel couldn't help grinning. He had a feeling he was going to like this woman. The engaging way she combined flippant flirtation with elegant sophistication settled one or two of the butterflies swarming around in his stomach.

She swept open the mahogany doors and he followed her into a spacious, richly adorned room. In the center of the room, two Queen Anne sofas dressed in silken ivory faced each other over an ornately carved coffee table. On one side of the sofas, a mahogany baby grand stood in the slanted light of two tall-paned windows dressed in red velvet. On the other side, floor-to-ceiling shelves offered a versatile library of books.

"I'll go get Sa—" She paused an instant. "Excuse me, *Lydia*." With that, she turned and left the room.

Daniel drew in a deep breath and released it through pursed lips. The moment he'd hoped, longed, and prayed for over the past five years was finally within his grasp.

He paced the floor for a couple of minutes, glancing at the open doorway every ten seconds or so. Then he wandered to one of the tall windows next to the piano. To his far right, he noticed a well-tended flower garden. A hungry bird, pecking away at lunch, perched on the lip of a cedar bird feeder that served as a centerpiece for a circle of impatiens. Bits and pieces of seed husks drifted down like snowflakes to the colorful blossoms below.

One corner of Daniel's mouth tipped upward. Lydia liked flowers—the ones with long stems or in vases, the kind he used to send her in celebration of a special day.

All at once, gooseflesh raced across the back of his neck. Slowly, expectantly, he turned, and the vision before him stole his breath.

Her free-flowing brown curls fell in a soft cloud around her face and shoulders. Her delicate skin glowed with candescent purity. Her amber eyes captured his soul.

Was this really Lydia?

Her heart-shaped face and petite build matched that of his beloved, but that's where the likeness ended. All the classic professionalism that represented Lydia's ambitious character—highlighted hair blown and gelled straight and turned under at the shoulders, enough makeup to camouflage what she considered every minor flaw, a form-fitting business suit and matching pumps—were all gone.

This woman was dressed in a simple salmon-pink dress that molded her tiny waist, then blossomed into a full skirt of countless crinkling folds that flowed freely over her slim hips and swirled around her tiny ankles, exposing only her small, ivory-slippered feet. No long, polished fingernails. No jewelry, except a basic gold-tone watch with a white leather band. Her earrings, if she wore any, were hidden by her hair.

While Daniel thought this sprite of a woman charming, he knew, beyond a fraction of a doubt, Lydia would never dress in such a down-to-earth and casual way.

Had he been wrong? Had he come here with high hopes only to find the wrong woman?

He knew exactly how to find out. He took a guarded step forward.

❧

As he came nearer, Sara clasped her hands tighter to keep them from shaking. Since last night, she had imagined what this moment would be like at least a hundred times. But not even in her most vivid dreams had she captured the reality.

His mere presence was overpowering; it wrapped around her like a warm blanket after a long, cold walk in the rain. His hopeful expression drew her. His seeking brown eyes mesmerized her.

How did I survive these last five years without you?

The thought stole into her mind, scattering her rehearsed reserve. When he stopped with a meager foot between them, she had to remind herself to breathe. He said nothing, just stood staring at her. When the weight of his perusal became more than she could bear, she bit her lower lip and ducked her head.

She watched his right hand rise slowly, felt his forefinger curl beneath her chin. He lifted her head until she once again looked into those penetrating dark eyes.

"Smile for me," he said.

His voice tremored, and her heart contracted. But his

request baffled her. She searched his face, then opened her mouth to ask *Why?*

"*Please*," he said, intercepting her intended question. "I just. . .need. . .to see you smile."

Her forehead creased. How could she smile on command?

Then she thought of the thing most precious to her, her daughter, and her lips curved of their own volition.

His gaze dropped to her chin, then slipped up to a spot an inch below the right corner of her mouth. She knew what had drawn his attention—a misplaced dimple, a unique oddity she never thought about until someone mentioned it. When he lifted his gaze back to hers, the tears in his eyes rocked her.

"Lydia," he whispered on a breath of wonderment. "It *is* you."

In less than a heartbeat, she found herself enveloped in his arms. His warm, male scent wrapped around her. She turned her head so that the side of her face rested on his chest. His racing heart kept pace with her own.

Her arms, with a sudden will of their own, rose and slipped beneath his blazer and around his waist. Her hands spread over the smooth material of the polo shirt that covered his muscular back. He buried his face in her hair and cupped the back of her head with one hand. A sob escaped his throat, shuddered through his body. . .and into hers.

Tears pushed against the back of her eyes as something strange, something wonderful flowed through her. Not a spark of recognition or even a trace of familiarity. Instead, she felt a long-awaited sense of belonging.

But her sanguine thoughts were shattered when he eased back, braced her head with his hands, and hungrily covered her mouth with his own.

❧

She pushed so hard against his chest, he stumbled backward. The outward curve of the baby grand bit into his hip, saving him from falling, and the wide-eyed terror on her face and the trembling hand pressed against her chest brought him reeling back to his senses.

"I'm sorry," he said. "I shouldn't have done that."

She didn't move, didn't speak. Just stared at him in stunned silence. Reaching out a hand, he took one cautious step forward.

She took a defensive step back, halting his advance.

He let his hand fall limply to his side. "I truly am sorry. It's just that the shock of seeing you again overwhelmed me."

"It's okay," she said, although her shaky voice betrayed her wariness. "It's just that. . .I don't know you."

The meaning of her words slammed into him, clipping the wings of hope that had carried him since that morning, when he'd first heard her voice on his cell phone. She did not know him; therefore, she did not love him anymore. Some of his most treasured remembrances were of her—but her memories of him, of what they once had. . .were gone.

He'd shared her past, but what about her future?

❧

With one shaky hand pressed against her stomach and the other against her chest, she willed her racing heart to slow down. She wasn't sure what shocked her most, being kissed by a man she'd met less than ten minutes ago, or her reaction to it. The second his lips had touched hers she'd been swept away by a heady sensation. She wasn't some wanton strumpet ready to fall into the arms of the nearest handsome man. At least, she didn't think she was.

When she felt she could speak again without stuttering, she swallowed and wet her tingling lips. "Why don't we sit down?"

He nodded, then waited while she perched on one end of the sofa like a nervous bird ready to take flight. He eased down next to her, settling back and crossing an ankle over the opposite knee.

How did he manage to look so composed after what had

just happened between them? Had the kiss not shaken him as it had her? Apparently not, if appearances were anything to go by.

For a few tense seconds, she studied the hands she'd clasped in her lap; then she lifted her gaze to find his intense brown eyes on her. Releasing a shuddery breath, she raised her hand and tucked a curl behind her ear, then dropped her hand back to her lap. "I think we've just established that this is going to be a challenge for us."

A rakish grin pulled at one corner of his mouth. "Like starting over."

He said the very words circling in her mind. But she wasn't ready to broach the details of their relationship just yet. She wanted to start with something safe, something still detached from her addled emotions.

"Tell me about Quinn Island," she said. "And my family."

Lacing his hands over his stomach, he stared into space for a few seconds, apparently trying to decide where to begin. "Quinn Island consists of one small barrier island and about twenty-five thousand acres inland," he said at last. "It was named for its founder, Samuel Quinn. Actually, you're a direct descendent. He was your grandfather—ten greats back, I think—but I tend to lose count on about the fourth great."

She found herself smiling at his wit.

"He and his family sailed to the East Coast from Ireland early in the eighteenth century," he added.

"You mean my family has lived there almost three hundred years?"

"That's right. Although the only true Quinns living among the island residents now are your father's and his brother's families."

"Why's that?"

"The town lost many residents to malaria during the 1700s, when the rice crops were so prosperous. Then many more moved away when the Civil War and a series of hurricanes halted rice production in the late nineteenth century. But time passed, newcomers moved in, and now Quinn Island is a thriving little town by the sea."

As he continued telling her about her heritage, her home, and her family, his smooth southern drawl served as an antidote to the anxiety that had been growing inside her since the night before. She found herself relaxing, settling back at an angle to face him, one arm folded across the top of the sofa and one leg curled beneath her.

When he described the barrier island, she grew a little breathless. She could almost feel the cool damp sand beneath her feet, smell the salt in the air, feel the breeze tug at her hair. Almost picture herself there. Almost, but not quite.

"It sounds so beautiful," she said when he finally paused.

"It is." His grin sent a flutter through her stomach. "Actually, you own a beach house on the island."

"I do?"

He nodded. "Your late Grandfather Quinn left it to you seven years ago."

"And I lived there?"

His smile waned. "No. You preferred living inland. You rented a townhouse apartment in town, near your shop."

That bit of information surprised her. For the last five years, she'd lived with the dream of living on a beach. As he talked more, she worried her lower lip with her teeth and focused blankly on the space beyond his right shoulder. Apparently, a lot had changed, but the biggest truth staring her in the face was how much *she* had changed. Had she really been the sophisticated southern belle Daniel spoke of with such affection?

"Lydia?"

His soft voice penetrated her thoughts. "Yes," she responded hesitantly. Answering to "Lydia" made her feel uneasy, like she was infringing on someone else's identity.

Twin lines creased his forehead. "You don't have to talk

about it now, if you don't want to, but I was wondering. . ." He swallowed, as if the rest of the sentence was lodged in the back of his throat.

She thought she knew what he wanted to ask. "You want to know what happened that night."

He answered with a somber nod.

"I really don't know. All I can tell you is what the doctors and police told me."

He reached over and wrapped his hand around one of hers, caressing her knuckles with his thumb. "Lydia, you don't have to—"

"No. It's okay. You need to know."

❧

Daniel's chest tightened with anticipation. He waited in silence for her to continue.

Finally, she pulled in a deep breath. "My first memory is of a faint beeping sound, which I later learned was a heart monitor. Then pain. Deep, heavy pain all over my body and inside my head."

He tightened his hold on her hand, but she didn't seem to notice.

"When the doctor managed to get some of the pain under control, I realized I was in a hospital. I asked him what I was doing there. He told me I had suffered severe trauma as the result of a physical assault. He asked if I remembered what happened to me. Of course, I didn't.

"Then he asked my name, and I couldn't tell him that either." She pursed her lips. "That was the most frightening thing of all, not knowing who I was, where I came from, how I had gotten there. . ." She sighed. "It still frightens me sometimes."

Her lips drew downward in a thoughtful frown. "When the doctor realized I couldn't remember anything, he explained I had been brought into the hospital two weeks earlier, unconscious and barely alive. I had been beaten and apparently left for dead."

"Who brought you into the hospital?"

"A truck driver, a man named Peter Maulding from Mobile, Alabama, found me at a rest stop just outside Chicago. He'd stopped to stretch his legs, and when he went to throw a coffee cup away, he noticed a bloody blanket rolled up around a large bundle inside the dumpster. When he looked closer, he saw a lock of my hair sticking out of one end. He called for help on his truck radio. The ambulance and police came and took me to the hospital."

Chewing on her lower lip, she glanced away. "The nurses said Mr. Maulding called every day to check on me. I finally got to talk to him a week after I regained consciousness. I thanked him for saving me. He simply said 'God be with you, ma'am,' and hung up. He never called back after that."

Daniel made a mental note to locate Peter Maulding and send the truck-driving angel of mercy his own personal "thanks."

"It took thirty-two stitches here," she continued, cupping the back of her head with her free hand. "And fifty-three here." Twisting around, she pushed back her thick curls, offering him a view of her left temple, where a jagged scar fanned out in several directions, like a web spun by a drunken spider. One rough side of the scar disappeared into her hairline.

She pulled her hair back over her temple, expertly concealing the blemish; a move, Daniel suspected, she'd practiced a million times over.

"There were other injuries. A lot of bruises, broken ribs, a broken shoulder, a collapsed lung. . ."

The more she told him about what some demented monster had done to her, the less he wanted to hear. When he felt he could bear no more, he searched his mind for a way to steer the conversation in another direction.

"How did you come to live with Mrs. Porter?" he asked when she paused to take a breath.

A smile touched her lips. "She was an auxiliary volunteer at the hospital. Still is. She visited me every day from the start. The nurses said she would talk to me, just like I was alert and could hear her, and she read passages to me from her Bible. They also said she prayed for me, for my healing.

"The visits continued after I woke, even though I was bitter and angry and not very pleasant company at first. I was so mad at God for allowing me to lose everything, even though I didn't know what it was I'd lost, I wanted no part of hearing that He loved me." A soft sigh drifted from her. "But Mrs. Porter was a stickler. She would say, 'Don't you worry, my dear. God and I are going to love that hate right out of you heart.' "

"And did they?"

Her delicate features softened even more. "Yes, they did. And when I was ready to leave the hospital and had no place to go, Mrs. Porter brought me here and nursed me back to health. When I got my strength back, she helped me find work."

"What kind of work?"

"Housework. I clean houses around the neighborhood four days a week. Fridays, I work here."

Daniel wouldn't have believed it if the words hadn't come from Lydia's own mouth. He couldn't think of an immediate response, so he simply stared at her.

She tipped her head to one side. "You look surprised."

"I am," he blurted, then shook his head to clear the fog that had gathered there. "I mean, someone called in during the program last night and said you looked like her cleaning lady, but I thought surely she was mistaken."

"Who was it?"

"A woman name Elizabeth Bradford."

"Yes." Lydia nodded. "I clean her house on Wednesdays. She lost her husband last year and she's having a hard time adjusting."

"Then you really do clean houses for a living?"

"Yes, I do."

He must have looked as dumbfounded as he felt, because after studying his face a couple of seconds, she said, "Why does that shock you so?"

"Because you hate housework. You used to hire someone to clean your shop and apartment once a week so you wouldn't have to do it yourself."

"Maybe I just didn't know how good I was at it."

"Are you saying you like it?"

She shrugged. "I can't complain. It keeps food on the table and a roof over our heads."

Another jolt of surprise pushed his eyebrows halfway up his forehead. "Our? You mean you keep up this entire house and feed yourself and Mrs. Porter on what you make cleaning houses?"

Her eyes widened and her mouth fell open.

Daniel's trained lawyer's eye read the expression. She'd let something slip unintentionally. He waited to see if she would explain.

She blinked, which seemed to snap her out of her stupefaction. "No. Mrs. Porter is financially secure. I merely rent two rooms from her for me and someone else."

A sharp, foreboding fear shot through Daniel. Was there another man? He'd never even considered the possibility.

Pulling her hand free from his, she leaned forward and opened a small coffee table drawer. Daniel held his breath. He felt like a loaded gun was pointed at his chest—and Lydia's finger was on the trigger.

She withdrew a picture in a gilded frame. Closing the drawer, she held the photo out to him. "This is Chloe."

With an unsteady hand, he reached for the frame. He found himself looking down at the image of a blond-haired, blue-eyed little girl with the face and smile of an angel. He felt his lips curve. "She's beautiful."

"She's my daughter."

His gaze snapped up to Lydia's. "Yours?"

She inclined her head. "She was born almost eight months after I was brought into the hospital. The doctors estimated she was one month premature."

Daniel tried to recover from the blow she had just delivered. She had a child. A daughter. How could that be?

She dropped her gaze to her lap and fidgeted with the creases in her skirt. "Daniel, ever since last night, I've wondered. . ." She pursed her lips, wet them, then swallowed. "I, ah, need to know. . ." Raising her lashes, she searched his face with beseeching brown eyes. "Could she be yours?"

Her question took him aback—and wounded his pride. "How could you even ask such a thing?"

She flinched like he'd raised a hand to strike her, and he would have given anything to take his sharp retort back.

"Lydia, I'm sorry." He reached for her hands. "For a second there, I forgot you couldn't remember."

"It's okay." She tugged one hand free from his and dabbed at a tear in the corner of her eye. "I just. . .needed to know for sure."

"No," he rasped, "she can't be mine. We were. . .are both Christians who had decided—well, we were going to wait until we married."

She bit her lower lip. A teardrop escaped, rolled down her cheek, and splattered his hand.

Cruel fingers of dread cut off the air in his lungs. *No, God, no! Please! Not Lydia!* A sick feeling churned in his stomach and burned his chest. He squeezed his eyelids shut. "You were. . ."

"Raped," she said in not much more than a whisper, supplying the word he couldn't speak. She followed up with an even softer "Yes."

Over the past five years, he had considered the possibility of a sexual assault. But since that morning, he had been so caught up in the joy of finding her. . .

The pain sweeping though him was more, much more than he'd ever imagined. If only he had been there. . . An almost unbearable weight bore down on his chest. He *should* have been there.

He felt her slim hand slide over his. "I'm sorry, Daniel. I just needed to know."

The coolness of her touch, like an early summer rain, and the sincerity in her voice, as though she owed him an apology, jerked him back from the dark hole into which he was slipping. He opened his eyes and looked into her solemn face. *Lord, if there is ever a time You're going to give me strength, please let it be now.*

He cradled her wet cheek in his palm. "No, Lydia. I'm the one who's sorry." He enfolded her in his arms. "This should not have happened to you."

If she wondered why, she didn't ask. She just slipped her arms up around his neck.

Cupping the back of her head with one hand, he buried his face in her sweet-smelling hair and began to rock her. "I am so, so sorry," he repeated.

But his words did nothing to ease the self-condemnation he felt. All the "I'm sorry's" in the world could never undo what he had let happen to her.

four

Lydia reined in her raw emotions. What was she doing, falling to pieces all over Daniel this way? Hadn't she known, deep down, that he wasn't Chloe's father? If the timing of her daughter's birth hadn't been enough to convince her, the sharp contrast between Chloe's fair complexion and Daniel's dark one should have been.

Still, since learning she had been engaged to him, a small part of her had hoped Chloe could be his, had yearned to know her child had been conceived in love and not violence. On the other hand, another part of her had feared if he were Chloe's biological father, the relationship could complicate things in the long run. She certainly didn't want Chloe trapped in the middle of a custody battle between an amnesiac mother and a father she didn't know.

Lydia released a shuddery sigh. At least she could find one consolation in confirming her daughter wasn't Daniel's child: She had been a woman of moral character, engaged to a man of honor. A deep sense of loss for what might have been, what would never be, washed over her.

Realizing she needed distance in order to regain her equilibrium, she forced her silent tears to ebb as she pushed away from him. She brushed at the shoulder of his sports coat as though the busy friction of her fingers would dry the dampness there. "I'm sorry. I didn't mean to cry all over you."

He captured a lingering tear with his thumb. A small gesture, but it almost unraveled her barely garnered emotions all over again.

"It's okay," he said. "It's turning out to be quite an eventful day for you. I think you're entitled."

41

Eventful didn't touch it. Spectacular. Out of the ordinary. All the things she thought she'd missed over the past five years rolled into one single day. How could she have ever thought she'd be ready for this moment? For facing her past? For a man like Daniel?

"Is she here?"

Daniel's question seemed misplaced, like he'd pulled it out of a trivia hat.

"Who?" Lydia asked, trying to think past the fog swimming around her brain.

"Chloe. I'd like to meet her."

"Oh."

Snapping back to reality, she stepped away, forcing Daniel to drop his hand from her face. She combed nervous fingers through her thick mane. "She's upstairs with Mrs. Porter. I'll go get her."

As soon as she was out of his sight, she once again pressed a hand to her quivering stomach. She couldn't believe the effect meeting him was having on her. The moment she had walked into the living room and he turned, looking at her with those dark eyes, she had felt a connection. Was it possible some dormant emotion from her past had been rekindled, even though she couldn't remember him? Or was she simply feeling the need to fill the unsatisfied longing that had grown over the last five years, the need to belong somewhere, to someone?

She hadn't known Daniel Matthews long enough for it to be anything more.

She found Chloe rocking in Evelyn Porter's lap, listening to a story.

" 'The sky is falling! The sky is falling!' " Mrs. Porter's voice hip-hopped through the air.

Henny Penny doesn't have a thing on me, Lydia thought, stepping farther into the room. Her world couldn't be any more precarious right now if the sky really was falling.

"Chloe, are you ready to go meet Mr. Matthews?"

"Yes!" Chloe pushed aside the book and scrambled down from Mrs. Porter's lap, the ever-present George the Giraffe tucked under her arm. Ever since Lydia had talked to her daughter that morning about Daniel, the curious tyke couldn't wait to meet "a man Mommy knew before moving to Chicago."

Lydia straightened Chloe's hair bow while she delivered a lecture on the appropriate times to say "please" and "thank you." Then, after a quick inspection to see if the child's green empire-waist dress, white tights, and black patent leather slippers were still clean and intact, she grasped her daughter's hand and headed for the door.

As they descended the steps, the flutter in Lydia's stomach increased. What would Daniel think of Chloe? Could he learn to love this innocent child created out of an act of black rage? Or would he ultimately reject her?

Lydia paused outside the living room, looked down at her daughter, and gave the tiny hand inside hers a reassuring squeeze. Then, squaring her shoulders, she opened the door.

Daniel stood waiting for them beside the sofa, his hands tucked casually inside his pockets. His gaze met Lydia's briefly, then dropped to Chloe.

Lydia felt an insistent tug on her hand. At her daughter's silent prompting, she stopped just a few feet inside the door. The next move would have to be Daniel's.

He came forward slowly, his attention fixed on Chloe.

The child rarely met anyone outside her sheltered world within the neighborhood. What would she do? Hide behind her mother's skirt? Run? To Lydia's amazement, Chloe stood statue still, her huge blue eyes gauging Daniel's every move.

He got down on one knee and looked into her eyes. "You must be Chloe."

Still clutching George beneath her arm, Chloe gave an emphatic nod.

"Your mom's been telling me about you. I'm Daniel."

"My mama said your name was 'Mr. Matthews.' "

Lydia's lips twitched, and a chuckle escaped Daniel's throat.

Resting his forearm across his raised knee, he said, "Only to people who aren't my friends. But I can already tell you and I are going to be very good friends, which means you can call me 'Daniel.' What do you think?"

Like a rehearsed act, both faces tilted upward and two beseeching gazes locked on Lydia's.

She was a stickler for manners and respect, and she didn't want Chloe to get in the habit of calling her elders by their first name. But with the pair looking up at her like two kids campaigning for an ice cream cone, she felt her resistance slip away. "Sure." She knew when she was defeated.

Chloe gave Daniel her most charming smile. "She says I can call you 'Daniel.' " In the same breath, she added, "Will you come play in my sandbox with me?"

Before Lydia could protest, Daniel was standing and lifting Chloe to his hip. "Sure, I will." He passed George to Lydia.

She stood, mouth agape, the giraffe with a bad hairdo dangling from her hand. She wanted to remind Chloe that she had on her best Sunday dress, and Daniel that he had on a pair of professionally creased Docker pants and what looked to her like an expensive pair of penny loafers. But the words froze in her muddled brain.

She wasn't so surprised at Daniel being enamored with Chloe. Once the child warmed up to someone—and she had warmed up to Daniel in record time—she had a charming personality that drew people to her.

But what was it about Daniel that had allowed him to slip so easily past Chloe's usual reserve? He'd waltzed right up to the child and, in the space of a minute, maybe two, swept the little girl off her feet.

Like mother, like daughter. The old cliché popped into Lydia's head, poking fun at her usual levelheadedness.

But Lydia and Chloe weren't the only ones who had fallen prey to Daniel's magnetic charm. Mrs. Porter had raved about him, too. She had said, *"He's got to be one of the most engaging young men I've ever met,"* when she came upstairs to fetch Lydia after showing him in.

First Mrs. Porter, then Lydia, now Chloe. Did the man affect the entire female population this way?

He stopped before opening the door Chloe had pointed him to and turned. "Coming, Mom?"

Realizing her mouth still hung open, she snapped it shut. "Ah, yes. I'm coming." George in tow, she hurried to catch up with them.

Thirty minutes later, she sat on the steps of the patio, chin in hand, her long skirt draped over her feet and legs, watching Daniel and Chloe. At first, Lydia had contemplated joining them, then decided the four-by-four sandbox made of scrap lumber she'd salvaged during a neighbor's renovation was barely big enough for two playmates, especially when one was a guesstimated six-foot-two man.

Daniel and Chloe shoveled sand and built imaginary houses where imaginary stick people lived. They laughed and giggled. The well-dressed attorney who had stepped into hers and Chloe's lives less than two hours ago didn't seem to mind one bit that the seat of his pants and the soles of his polished cordovan shoes were nestled in gritty, clingy sand.

He had shucked off his blazer and tossed it over a nearby swing seat, revealing lean, muscled forearms beneath the sleeves of his white polo shirt. Whenever he tilted his head a certain way, the afternoon sun lit the chestnut highlights in his dark hair. Every once in a while, his laughter floated through the air, each time touching a place inside her she hadn't even known existed. He looked like a man in his element, a man carved by God's own hand for fatherhood.

Lydia realized where her thoughts were drifting, and she mentally rebuked her wandering mind. She could chase dreams of Chloe being Daniel's daughter until the sun set in the east. The truth remained that Daniel was not, and never would be, Chloe's biological father. Considering the circumstances of Chloe's conception, it would take a mighty big man to overcome that obstacle and accept the child as his own.

And this early in the game, Lydia didn't know if Daniel was quite big enough.

&

An hour later, after tucking Chloe in for her afternoon nap, Lydia stepped outside her daughter's room ahead of Daniel. With little effort, Chloe had talked him into picking up where Mrs. Porter had left off reading *Henny Penny*. Then she had fallen asleep in his lap.

Lydia waited for the faint click of the closing door. "Chloe's quite taken with you," she said.

He grinned. "I'm quite taken with her."

Trapping her lower lip between her teeth, she looked down the hallway at nothing in particular. They had so many things to discuss. So many circumstances to consider. "You understand now why I didn't want any attention drawn to your finding me."

"To protect Chloe?" he guessed correctly.

Nodding, she turned her attention back to him. "I know the chances are slim, but if one of the men who attacked me—"

His eyebrows shot up. "Men? You mean there was more than one?"

Lydia closed her eyes ruefully and pressed a cool palm to her forehead. She kept letting things slip before she was ready to talk about them. Was she losing her mind now along with her identity?

Dropping her hand, she lowered her gaze to the base of his neck exposed by the V-opening of his collar. "Yes. The doctors said there were at least two." When she raised her lashes, he looked away, but not before she caught the pain in his eyes.

She knew, in many ways, his grief cut deeper than hers. He had lost someone very dear to him the night of her abduction. But she had no memory of the attack. When she talked about it, she felt as though she were talking about someone else, someone she'd read about in the newspaper or seen on the evening news but never met. She couldn't feel the fear, the horror, the pain she must have felt that night. Besides the physical scars her body carried, the only evidence left that such a violent act had been committed against her was something very dear to her—her daughter.

"Would you like some tea?" she suggested. She and Daniel could both use a break, take some time to calm their frazzled nerves before talking about the next step they should take.

Daniel nodded, then followed her downstairs and into the kitchen.

⠆⠄

Fury almost choked him. He wanted revenge on the demons who had violated Lydia. Even as his inner voice told him his thoughts were immoral, he envisioned himself torturing the life out of each faceless monster.

She refused his offer of help, so he pulled out a chair, sat down, and watched her flutter around the kitchen like an energetic butterfly. She filled a teakettle with water and placed it on the stove, then reached into the cupboard and pulled out two ceramic cups.

"We have chamomile and regular," she said. "Which would you like?"

Since he didn't know what chamomile was, he decided to play it safe. "Regular."

"Cold or hot?"

"Cold." Five years ago, she had known that.

"Sweetened? Unsweetened? Cream? Lemon?"

She threw the single-word questions at him like he was a dartboard, and he felt himself smile. She looked so captivating, standing there holding the cups against her chest like two cuddly kittens, her amber eyes wide in anticipation of his answer.

"Sweet," he said, referring to more than the tea. "No cream or lemon."

She had also known he didn't take cream or lemon in his tea five years ago, a little irritating voice inside reminded him, tempering the joy he felt at simply watching her putter around the kitchen. How was it that practically everything she did reminded him she couldn't remember him or what they had once shared, yet at the same time, charmed him so? In some ways, he felt like he was experiencing the rapture of falling in love all over again. In other ways, he felt as though he were groping in the dark, wondering which way to turn, what to reach for.

She set his iced tea in front of him, then returned to the counter where she added a teaspoon of honey and a tea bag to a cup of boiling water. Balancing the cup over a saucer, she padded to the table. "Would you like something to eat? I can fix you a sandwich."

He'd missed lunch, but the way he felt right now, his appetite might not ever return. "No, thank you. Tea's fine."

He waited until she sat down, then lifted his drink in a mock salute before taking a long, cool sip. When he set his dewy glass back down, he watched as she dipped her tea bag in and out of the steaming liquid in her cup. The water, he noticed, was turning a color that reminded him of stagnant pond water. Finally, she laid the bag on the edge of the saucer and took a careful sip of the pungent-smelling brew.

"What kind of tea did you say that was?" he asked as she settled the cup back in its saucer.

"Chamomile. It's supposed to have a calming effect." She shrugged one shoulder. "Most of the time it works."

Maybe that's what he should have had. He studied the fog rising from the cup, debating on changing his mind—until he caught another whiff of the acrid-smelling liquid. *Nope,* he decided without further contemplation. That chamomile stuff reminded him of the rabbit tobacco he and his cousins used to sneak to their grandpa's woodshed to chew during their rambunctious adolescent years. The aftermath was never worth the effort. Retching had never been fun.

Besides, the only thing he drank hot was coffee.

The contrary little beast inside him nudged him again, pointing out that Lydia had never cared for hot tea either. Water and diet soda had been the only liquid she'd ever let pass through her painted lips.

His gaze slid to her mouth. Those lips weren't painted at all right now, just barely moistened by a trace of the sheer gloss she'd been wearing when he first arrived. He had to admit, he liked them that way.

He took another long drink of tea, then studied the dew beading on his glass while he tried to collect his scattered senses. How could one experience so many conflicting emotions at once? Joy and sorrow. Pleasure and pain. Courage and fear.

So far, he'd found only a remnant of what he'd lost five years ago, and he didn't know if that was good. . .or bad.

ð

Lydia set her teacup in its saucer and studied Daniel. He looked so sad with his head bowed and his gaze fixed on his half-empty glass. What was he thinking? After learning all that had happened to her, was he sorry he'd found her? Was he tormented by what the attack had cost her? Cost him?

He'd said they were both Christians and had decided to wait until their wedding night to claim each other as one. He had been a man of honor about to marry a woman of purity. Lydia suspected he was still a man of honor, but she was no longer a woman of purity. And that was only one cold, harsh fact wedged between them. There would, she suspected, be many, many more.

Above all, there was Chloe. Right now, Daniel was caught up in the thrill of finding *Lydia*. But what about later, when the excitement of new beginnings died and the dust of celebration settled? Would he be reminded of how Chloe had been conceived every time he looked at her?

Was finding out worth the risk?

Lydia reached over and laid her palm on Daniel's forearm.

When he looked up, the anguish in his eyes almost made her look away. Almost. But she somehow hung on to her resolve and pushed forward. "Daniel, I truly am sorry."

He frowned. "What for?"

"For all the terrible things you're finding out about me. That I'm not the same woman I was five years ago."

Abruptly, he stood. Caught off guard by the sudden action, she flinched. The heavy oak chair upset by the impact of the back of his knees teetered on its hind legs for a few precarious seconds, then settled with a dull thud on all fours.

Before Lydia could react, he captured her upper arms in his firm yet tender grip and lifted her. The space between their bodies vanished as she gaped up at him in surprise. He looked down at her with a turbulent expression in his eyes she couldn't define. Each of his breaths brushed her face like a swiftly passing storm.

"Lydia, what happened to you was not your fault!" he said through clenched teeth. "Do you hear me? It was *not. . .your. . . fault*." He punctuated each of his last three words with a gentle shake.

Then, as swiftly as the storm came, it dissipated. His features softened and his eyes filled with. . .compassion, sorrow, remorse? She wasn't sure. She just knew the entire atmosphere changed from turbulent to tender in less than a second.

"It's not your fault," he repeated, each breath now touching her face as soft as a whisper. "And it doesn't change the person you are." He shook his head, gazing down at her in a way that made her feel like she had just stepped into a beautiful dream. "It doesn't change a thing, Lydia. Especially the way I feel about you."

He gathered her in his arms, cupped the back of her head with one hand, nestled her cheek against his chest. "I love you, Lydia. I always have. I always will."

She knew he meant it, just as sure as she knew the arms holding her were sincere, and the hands caressing her would never harm her. Regardless of what had happened, he still loved her and was willing to go the distance.

But was she?

She didn't know. She was afraid of getting hurt, of hurting Chloe. . .of hurting him.

She slipped her arms around his waist and allowed his strength to surround her. Each rise and fall of his chest, every heartbeat, seemed to mirror her own. Her resistance was gone, had vanished like a bad dream at dawn the moment he said, "I love you." What in the world was she going to do?

She released a shuddery sigh. "I can't pick up where we left off," she heard herself say. "You know that, don't you, Daniel?"

"I know." He drew back and braced her face with hands neither too big nor too small, neither too rough nor too smooth. "We'll start over, and take it slow." He caressed her cheek with his thumb. "You're my destiny, Lydia. We were meant to be together."

A look of deep longing rose in his eyes, igniting inside her a desire to fulfill his dreams. The atmosphere grew still, and for a moment they did nothing but stare at each other. Then his gaze dropped to her mouth. Her heartbeat accelerated in anticipation of his kiss—and the knowledge that when it came, she'd be powerless to resist.

But it never came. Instead, he simply slipped his arms around her again and held her. She marveled at the incredible feeling of being embraced by a man who loved her enough to remain loyal through five long years of separation.

But would that love survive the future? He'd said nothing had changed, but she knew it had. And he knew it, too, even if he wasn't yet ready to admit it. A chilly finger of foreboding brushed her spine, intruding on her moment of bliss, reminding her of the stark reality anchored to their reunion.

He remembered the woman she was.

She knew only the woman she'd become.

What they once had was gone.

Once Daniel figured that out, would he still think of her as his destiny?

five

Much later that evening, Daniel all but collapsed when he sat down on the freshly made brass bed. When he'd earlier mentioned finding a motel room, Mrs. Porter had insisted he stay in one of the two empty bedrooms upstairs. He hadn't put up an argument—he wanted to stay as close to Lydia as possible.

He massaged the back of his neck where fibers of tension had gathered. He knew the night would bring little sleep, but he did need to get what rest he could. He hoped to get Lydia home by day after tomorrow, which meant tomorrow would be filled with hasty preparation.

But there was one task he couldn't postpone until morning. He fished his cellular phone out of his blazer pocket, flipped it open, and dialed. The phone on the other end rang once.

"Hello?" came the anxious voice of Margaret Quinn. "Daniel, is that you?"

"Yes, Margaret, it's me."

"Where on earth are you?" Lydia's mother wanted to know. "We called your office this afternoon and your secretary said there'd been a change in your plans. Did the television station receive any more calls after we spoke with you last night?"

Daniel decided to get right to the point. Lydia's parents had waited long enough for this call. "I'm in Riverbend, Illinois—"

"Illinois? Wha—"

"I've found Lydia."

Silence filled his ear, then a breathless, "Oh, dear heavenly Father," slipped from her lips. "Bill! Bill! Come quickly! Daniel's found Lydia! Where is she?" Margaret asked Daniel

52

next in the same breath. "Can I speak to her?"

"I'd rather you wait until tomorrow to do that."

"Tomorrow!" Her voice was appalled. "You can't be serious. Tell me how to get there. We'll take the first flight out."

"Before you do anything, Margaret, I need to tell you a few things."

Daniel heard a faint click. "Daniel?" came the slightly out-of-breath voice of Bill Quinn. "Is it true? Have you really found her?"

"Yes, Bill, it's true."

"Oh, thank God." The older man released a sob.

Bill's reaction played havoc with Daniel's overwrought emotions, which he'd barely managed to temper before making the call. He squeezed his burning eyes shut. He had to get this out. He had to somehow tell them about Lydia without breaking down again himself. *Help me, Lord,* he silently prayed, and a fragile but definite sense of calm stole over him.

"There are some things you need to know before you talk to her," he finally managed to say, and without hesitation he plowed ahead, telling them about her waking up in a Chicago hospital sixteen days after her disappearance, her amnesia, and how she came to live with Mrs. Porter. He finished with "She has a daughter. . .as a result of the ra—" he closed his eyes, forcing down a sudden wave of nausea, "—as a result of the attack."

"Oh, my baby," Margaret said in a raspy, choking voice. "My poor, poor baby."

"The little girl," Daniel added, barely holding onto his brittle composure. "Her name is Chloe."

"Chloe," Margaret repeated.

"That's right."

For five full seconds, Margaret Quinn said nothing, as though she were giving the child's name a chance to take root somewhere. Daniel prayed it would be in her heart.

"What does she look like?" she finally asked, unable to

disguise her concern and curiosity.

Daniel's anger at the torture Lydia had suffered returned, dropping on his chest like an exploding bomb that spread into each limb. "Not like Lydia." *And not me. She'll never look like me.* "But she's the most beautiful child I've ever seen," he added, and meant it.

Three seconds ticked away. "I'm sure she is, Daniel." The woman's timorous laugh brushed Daniel's ear. "What about that, Bill? We're grandparents."

Daniel breathed a sigh of relief. He couldn't help worrying about how Mrs. Quinn would take the news of Chloe. Margaret Quinn always had her family's best interest at heart, even when she was overbearing. But she sometimes focused too much on image and appearance, especially where her daughters were concerned.

"How is she, Daniel?" Bill cut in. "Is she there with you? When can we talk to her?"

"Physically, she's fine. Emotionally? I don't know. She seems to be okay, but quite honestly, it's too early for me to tell what kind of impact her memory loss has had on her. That's why I wanted to prepare you before you speak with her. She doesn't remember anything or anyone from her past before the abduction, so, please, don't expect more from her than she's able to give right now. I know you're both anxious to see her, but I think it'd be best to wait until we get home."

"When will that be?" Margaret asked.

"Hopefully, in a couple of days. Another thing, she wants to return quietly. No hoopla and fanfare." This he said more to Lydia's mother than her unassuming father.

"But so many of her friends will want to welcome her home," Margaret argued, as Daniel had expected her to. She probably had half the homecoming party planned by now.

"In time, they can," he responded, unbending. "But it will have to be when Lydia's ready. Remember, she's coming back to a place and people she doesn't remember. That's overwhelming enough in itself."

"I think Daniel's right, Margaret," Bill injected, and Daniel silently thanked the older man. "Let's keep the homecoming limited to family for now."

"Okay," Margaret relented, albeit reluctantly. "If you think that's best, Daniel."

"I do." He raked his hair away from his forehead. A rebellious lock flopped back down over his left brow. "Listen, I'd better go. I'll call back first thing in the morning. If she's up to it, you can talk to her then."

After hanging up, Daniel sat for a long time with his elbows on his knees and his hands clasped in front of him, staring at the darkness beyond the bedroom window. For some reason, the words of an old song he associated with funerals came to mind.

> *Precious memories, unseen angels,*
> *Sent from somewhere to my soul;*
> *How they linger, ever near me,*
> *And the sacred past unfold.*

As he sat there, with the lines of that old hymn floating through his head, the past did unfold, memory by precious memory, starting with the first time Daniel noticed Lydia as more than another kid in the neighborhood. He'd been home on Thanksgiving break his fourth year in college and had attended a high school football game with a friend. Lydia had been seventeen then, captain of the cheerleading squad, and to Daniel, the most beautiful thing he'd ever seen.

At least a hundred more memories played themselves out in his mind: her college graduation, the day she opened her dress shop, the evening he proposed. Right up until the day she'd left for the fateful New York trip, pouting in that pretty way of hers because he wouldn't postpone his first solo court case to go with her.

When the reflections came to a haunting end, he dropped his forehead to his hands. A harrowing question preyed on his mind: Would things between him and Lydia ever be as they once were? An even more frightening question followed, casting shadows of doubt over the first: Did he even want to return to the life they'd once shared?

He gave his head a disparaging shake. He didn't know. He truly didn't know. He never imagined finding her would bring so much confusion. . .and pain. "Oh, God, help me," he pleaded. "Please, please help me."

Daniel didn't know exactly what he was asking for. Only that he would need guidance in the days to come from One much stronger than he.

When he finished praying, he closed his eyes and wept.

❧

Lydia Quinn, she said to herself for about the hundredth time in half as many hours. She tossed a pair of socks in the open suitcase on her bed. *Lydia Anne Quinn. Ms. Lydia Quinn.*

No matter how she rehearsed the name in her mind, it still sounded as foreign to her as the first time she'd heard it. She paused in packing and stepped in front of her dresser mirror, trying to picture herself as a sophisticated southern belle. Like the dozen or so other times she'd stood there since the day before yesterday, all she saw was "Sara," mother of Chloe, close friend and companion to Evelyn Porter.

Shaking her head, she went back to packing. How was she ever going to step back into her old shoes? This wasn't some fairy tale where the peasant heroine slipped on the glass slipper and found a perfect fit. This was her own life, and she had a feeling her shoe size had changed dramatically over the past five years.

When she closed the case, the latch caught with an amplified click of finality. Her life here was coming to an end. In less than an hour, she, Chloe, Mrs. Porter, and Daniel would leave for the airport. In less than two, they'd be on a flight to

Quinn Island—her home. She was so glad Daniel had invited Mrs. Porter to come along and stay for a few weeks. At least Lydia would have a confidant while she reacquainted herself with her family.

As she turned to her dresser and started tossing her meager toiletries into a makeup bag, her mind drifted back over the hours since Daniel had walked into her life. Yesterday had started out like a whirlwind. She had been moved by the conversations with her parents and sister over the telephone. Hearing the weepy joy in their voices was enough to toy with her own emotions. But that was it. She hadn't even been able to work up a tear at the prospect of returning home to these three people who obviously loved and missed her very much. A sigh escaped her lips. Surely, that would all change once she got to know them.

After the phone call, Lydia had made rounds in the neighborhood, saying good-bye and letting the families she worked for know Mrs. Porter's great-niece, a college student on summer break, would soon be taking over her cleaning jobs. By the time she returned, Daniel had booked a flight to Myrtle Beach International Airport, arranged to have a shuttle pick them up this morning and take them to O'Hare, and made plans to have Lydia's and Chloe's few material possessions— aside from their clothes—shipped to her parents' house.

Lydia wasn't quite sure how she felt about his assertive efforts. In some ways, she was grateful he was a take-action sort of guy. He had taken care of a dozen little details that would have been a bit overwhelming for her. After all, she was acquainted with very little of the world outside the subdivision she'd lived in for the past five years.

Even so, Daniel could have kept her better informed. Other than wanting to know how soon she could be ready to go home, he hadn't asked her opinion about anything. And that pricked an irritating little nerve in Lydia. She might have lost her memory, but she hadn't lost her mind. She still had the ability to think and make decisions for herself and her daughter.

She sensed another's presence and paused short of dropping her tube of lip gloss in the makeup bag. Even before looking toward the open doorway, she knew who she would find there. Deliberately, she set the lip gloss back on the dresser and closed her eyes, stealing a deep breath of fortitude. This was going to be the hardest good-bye of all.

Opening her eyes, she turned slowly to face the sad green eyes of her best friend. "Jeff," she whispered, and a lump lodged in her throat.

He stood with his hands shoved into the pockets of his khaki pants, his shoulders hunched forward. When their gazes met, he pursed his lips, and his chin quivered. Behind the lenses of his wire-rimmed glasses, his eyes grew misty. His desolate expression reflected the feeling rising in Lydia's chest. They had been through so much together, from the premature birth of her daughter, to the untimely death of his wife. And she would miss him—a lot.

But Lydia knew, as did he, things had changed. The love he had hoped would one day blossom between them would never come to pass.

"I'm going to miss you, kid," he said, his voice heavy with sorrow.

Three steps each and they were in each other's arms. "I'm going to miss you, too," she said.

"I love you. You know that, don't you?"

"I know. I love you, too."

But theirs was not the kind of love that made two people one—the kind he and his deceased wife had shared. And deep down, Lydia was sure he knew that, too.

❧

"I love you. You know that, don't you?"

"I know. I love you, too."

Daniel stopped short of stepping up to the open doorway

of Lydia's room. What was this? Lydia proclaiming her love to another man?

He leaned against the wall for support. Why hadn't she told him this before now?

A brief silence followed, leaving Daniel to wonder what was happening between them. Were they holding each other? *Kissing* each other? The image of Lydia locked in another man's lent new strength to Daniel's limbs. He'd just found her, and he had no intentions of losing her—again. He pushed away from the wall and stepped up to the open doorway, bracing himself for the scene he expected to find.

Lydia apparently caught his movement out of the corner of her eye and stepped away from the strange man. When she turned to face Daniel, he expected a look of guilt or embarrassment, an expression that said "I wish the floor would open up and swallow me." Instead, she greeted him with an innocent smile.

She tucked her hand into the crook of the stranger's arm, and together they stepped forward. "Daniel, I'd like you to meet a very dear friend of mine."

The man stretched out his right hand. "Jeff Chandler. It's nice to meet you."

Yeah, right, thought Daniel, as he returned the handshake. Either the man really *was* just a friend or he was an idiot. If he felt for Lydia half of what Daniel did, he'd be bracing himself for a battle, not shaking the enemy's hand.

With a curt nod, Daniel pumped the man's hand, once. "Daniel Matthews. Likewise."

"Yes, I saw you on *Without a Trace* the other night." Jeff pushed his glasses up the bridge of his nose, then stuffed his fists into his pockets. "Sara's waited a long time for this day. I know you're happy she's going home."

Lydia. Her name is Lydia. He slipped a possessive arm around her, urging her to step away from Jeff. Daniel feared she'd stiffen, pull away, send some sort of silent signal that she didn't want him showing such an open gesture of affection in front of her "dear friend."

But she didn't. In fact, he thought he felt her lean into him a little.

"Words can't express how happy I am," Daniel said. "Her parents and sister, too."

Jeff's gaze held Daniel's for a moment, and Daniel got the peculiar sensation that the man was trying to convey some sort of silent message. Then a look of sad resignation rose in Jeff's eyes, and, in spite of himself, Daniel felt a thread of sympathy for Lydia's friend.

"You're a fortunate man," Jeff said. He turned his attention to Lydia, and his features softened even more. "I'm going to go say good-bye to Chloe now." He leaned over, kissed Lydia's cheek, and squeezed her hand. "Take care, kid. You know where I am if you ever need me."

Lydia nodded, and even though she smiled, Daniel noticed tears gathering in her eyes.

Jeff turned and walked away, and for a moment, Daniel looked after him. What did the man really mean to Lydia?

She stepped away from him, taking her comforting warmth with her. When he focused his attention back on her, she was standing with her arms crossed, glowering at him like a first-grade teacher ready to go head-to-head with a willful student.

"How much of that conversation did you hear?" she asked.

He decided to play innocent, see how much information she would volunteer about her relationship with Jeff. "What do you mean?"

"I mean, you came in here like a man on a mission. And I'd like to know how much of my conversation with Jeff you listened in on."

He took a few seconds to size her up. In the past, she'd never been so direct. . .or insightful. He rubbed his jaw. The determination and challenge in her demeanor told him there was no point in trying to continue with his charade. She'd already seen through it.

"I heard him tell you he loves you," he admitted. And with that admission came a feeling Daniel hadn't experienced in a very long time. A slip in control. It felt strange. . .like a shoe on the wrong foot.

"Then you heard me tell him I love him, too."

He inclined his head.

"I do," she said.

Hearing her confess her love for another man while she was staring him down had more impact on him than when he was standing outside her door. He thought he'd suffocate right there on the spot.

"But I'm not *in love* with him," she added.

He arched an inquisitive brow. "Meaning. . .?"

She glanced away, a frown pinching her forehead. After a long, thoughtful moment, she looked back at him. "I met Jeff when I was in the hospital. His wife Caroline was one of my nurses."

Daniel perked up. Jeff had a wife. That was good.

"I don't know why they and Mrs. Porter chose to befriend me, but they did," Lydia continued. "They supported me emotionally while my body healed physically. They stood beside me during my pregnancy and Chloe's premature birth. They were, I suppose, a substitute family to me and Chloe."

An expression of deep pain clouded her delicate features. "Then the unthinkable happened and Caroline was diagnosed with Lou Gehrig's disease. I was with her and Jeff when she died eighteen months ago."

Now Daniel felt like a heel. The man had lost, big-time. A loss that, in many ways, Daniel could relate to.

Lydia drew in a deep breath, released it slowly. "After her death, I tried to help Jeff out with his kids when the burden of single fatherhood overwhelmed him. I tried to listen when he got so lonely for Caroline he thought he was going to die. I tried to be there for him, like he had been there for me.

"The kind of love Jeff and I share is the kind between two friends who have been to hell and back with each other." Her light brown eyes sought for understanding. "Haven't you ever had a friend like that?"

A picture of Lydia's sister Jen floated across his mind. They had gone through the heartbreak of Lydia's disappearance together, had grown closer through it. He had to admit he understood exactly what Lydia was trying to say.

"Yes, I have," he said, pulling her into his arms. Resting his chin on the top of her head, he added, "I'm sorry I jumped to the wrong conclusion."

"You don't owe me an apology, Daniel. Considering you didn't know the circumstances, I'm sure what you heard sounded suspicious."

"Still, I shouldn't have barreled in here like 'a man on a mission.' "

She drew back, smiling up at him. "I don't know. I found it kind of flattering, myself."

A pleased grin lifted one corner of his mouth. "You did?"

"Yes. I did."

Like a warm cloak in a chilly wind, the air grew heavy with enthralling tension. Slowly, their smiles faded. She wet her lips. Her involuntary movement drew his gaze to her mouth, and a shudder of longing shook him. He became aware of her every breath.

He lifted his eyes back to hers. "I guess you know I want to kiss you."

Releasing a pent-up breath, she pushed away. "Please don't. Thinking about going to Quinn Island and meeting my family has me addlepated enough as it is."

Addlepated. Now there was a word he'd never heard her use before. But he thought he knew what she meant.

Patting her chest like she was trying to calm an unsteady palpitation, she turned to her dresser. She dropped a tube of lip gloss into a makeup bag, zipped it, and tossed the bag into a small open suitcase on the bed. After securing the luggage, she straightened and turned back around to face him. "There's one other thing I need to tell you—"

Outside, a vehicle horn blared.

A rueful smile tipped her lips. "I guess it can wait. There's our ride to the airport."

She slipped the thin strap of her purse over her shoulder and reached for the luggage lying on the bed, but Daniel was one step ahead of her.

"I can at least carry the small one," she said.

"I've got it."

She nodded, offering no further argument.

Standing in the middle of the room, she took one last lingering look at her surroundings. Then, drawing back her shoulders, she lifted her chin a determined inch, forcing more courage into her actions than her anxious eyes reflected.

"Well," she said, "I guess it's time to go home."

six

"How many times have I done this before?" Lydia asked Daniel as she fastened her airplane seat belt with slightly shaky hands. A jittery knot bounced in her stomach.

"Five or six," Daniel answered, making sure Chloe was safely secured in her seat.

Daniel had been fortunate enough to reserve adjoining seats in the same row for him, Chloe, and Lydia. He—at Lydia's insistence—had taken the window seat, Chloe sat in the middle, and Lydia sat next to the aisle. She really wasn't interested in seeing how high the plane could fly.

Mrs. Porter sat in the aisle seat one row up.

Lydia rechecked Chloe's restraint. She knew Daniel had aptly secured the belt, but fidgeting gave her something to do with her hands besides wringing them in her lap. "Was I always this nervous?"

"A little the first time. But after that you always looked forward to the flight."

Mild turbulence during takeoff had Lydia clinging to her armrests; Chloe reached for Lydia. But once Daniel explained an airplane penetrating air pockets was like a pin popping balloons, Chloe found the occasional bump-bang rather amusing and began to giggle.

Lydia's uneasiness, however, didn't calm until the plane leveled off and the flight became smooth. Then, she realized, she didn't mind flying at all. She reminded herself of what Daniel had said about her enjoying flying in the past after she'd conquered her first-flight jitters. Maybe she had finally found something she had in common with her old self.

Her fit of anxiety returned full force when the pilot

announced they were approaching Myrtle Beach International Airport. Meeting people who knew more about her past than she did weakened her fortitude, made her feel as though the thin shell of her self-composure might break under the mildest look of criticism.

"Are you okay?" Daniel asked as the plane rolled to a stop.

Lydia met his gaze of concern. "A little nervous," she admitted. "I never realized meeting my own family would be so. . ."

"Scary?"

She forced a smile. "Yeah." Looking down at her daughter, she pasted on a cheery expression. "Are you ready to meet Grandma and Grandpa Quinn and your aunt Jennifer?"

With a sparkle in her eyes, Chloe bobbed her head and raised her arms so Daniel could unfasten her seat belt. They fell in line and shuffled down the aisle. Daniel, with Chloe perched on his hip, led the way since he was the only one familiar with the airport and its unloading routine. Lydia followed Daniel, and Mrs. Porter fell in behind.

Lydia forced herself not to withdraw while people of all shapes, sizes, and ages craned their necks in search of their loved ones. She scanned the colossal wall of faces, hoping to locate those waiting for her. Seeing them first would at least give her a chance to brace for their reaction.

A man in a dark suit, carrying a briefcase in one hand and holding a cellular phone to his ear with the other, breezed by, bumping Lydia's shoulder and, for an instant, he drew her attention away from the crowd.

"Hey, do you know how to say 'Excuse me'?" she heard Daniel say.

The busy man just shot Daniel a flippant glance and kept on going.

Lydia's lips pinched together. Sure, the man had been rude, but that was no reason to solicit a brawl in the middle of an international airport. She was going to have to talk to Daniel about his impetuous overprotection.

"There they are!" A female voice rose above the crowd. "Lydia! Lydia!"

Before Lydia could lock onto the source of the voice, she found herself clenched in a fierce embrace. A blanket of blond hair brushed her face. Her nostrils filled with the sweet fragrance of expensive perfume. She tilted her head so her chin could rest atop the woman's shoulder and reminded herself to hug this still unknown member of her family.

Just as quickly as she'd grabbed Lydia, the woman set her back, keeping a hold on her upper arms. Lydia found herself looking into the misty blue eyes of a slim young woman at least six inches taller than herself.

Jennifer. Her sister. Lydia recognized the sibling from *Without a Trace.*

"Oh, Lydia." Tears streaming, Jennifer lifted her hands to frame Lydia's face. "Look at you. You look wonderful."

Jennifer's gaze zipped to the area beyond Lydia's left shoulder. "And this must be Chloe."

As Jennifer stepped aside and flitted toward her niece, Lydia saw the couple who had been standing a few feet behind her sister. The woman leaned on a cane; the man held a protective arm around her. They were looking at Lydia like a young mother and father admiring their newborn for the first time after a long, complicated pregnancy.

"Mom? Dad?" Her voice was as small as a frightened child's. Lydia stepped forward at the same time they did, and they all came together in a fervent embrace.

Almost immediately, a warm feeling of acceptance stole over Lydia. She might not know these two people yet. Their faces might not be familiar to her as they once were, and their names might still sound strange and foreign. But one thing she did know—they loved her, as parents love their children. She could hear it in the tremble of their voices when they spoke to her, feel it in the strength of the arms as they held her.

Maybe she'd arrived "home" after all.

🙠

They claimed their luggage, then made their way out to the parking area where Daniel had left his sleek white sedan—a lawyer's car, for sure. They fastened Chloe's seat belt and then Daniel, Lydia, and Mrs. Porter got in his car with the child, while Bill, Margaret, and Jennifer left to retrieve Jennifer's car from another lot.

An hour later, Daniel turned onto a road marked Plantation Lane. He threw up his hand at the fourth deputy sitting in the fourth patrol car Lydia had noticed parked alongside the road since they'd entered the Quinn Island city limits ten minutes ago.

"Daniel," she queried, "are all these deputies for my benefit? Or is Quinn Island just well blessed with lawmen?"

"They're for your benefit and Chloe's. I called the sheriff yesterday and asked him to keep an eye out in case someone learned of your return. When the news starts spreading, it will draw a lot of attention. I didn't want you having to deal with that today."

"I appreciate that," she said. And she did appreciate his foresight—but not that he'd failed to inform her of his contact with the sheriff. She chewed her lower lip in frustration. What else had he failed to tell her?

"Also, Lydia," Daniel added, "I had to inform the sheriff you'd been found. Remember, you were the victim of a crime. There are going to be a lot of questions. . .interrogations in the days to come. I want you to be prepared for that." He glanced her way. "I'll be there with you through the whole thing. You'll not have to go through it alone."

Like ice cream in the summer sun, her irritation melted. She couldn't stay annoyed at him—he wouldn't let her. He was too gentle. Too kind. Too doggedly determined to look out for her and Chloe.

"Thank you," she told him. "That means a lot."

He turned his attention back to the road, and she turned hers to the roadside, where oleanders, palm trees, and other foliage that looked native to a tropical island lined the street. She made a mental note to ask Daniel the names of the plants she wasn't familiar with—and to buy a pair of dark sunglasses. The midafternoon sun seemed so much brighter here than in Chicago.

After they'd traveled about half a mile, Daniel turned the car onto a paved drive and stopped in front of a gate. When he pressed a button on a small box clipped to his sun visor, the black iron doors swung open. He maneuvered the vehicle through the gate, while Jennifer, Margaret, and Bill followed in Jennifer's car.

The narrow road was banked on each side by huge oaks. The branches of the mammoth trees, dripping with Spanish moss, offered a patchy overhead canopy that sprinkled the pavement with mottled shadows and sunshine.

They rounded a bend, and Lydia gasped in awe. The two-story brick house, a renovated and updated remnant of rice plantation days, with four heavy white columns and four second-story dormer windows, was like a regal queen on her throne. The house sat in the midst of acres of green lawn sparsely dotted with more oaks and native trees she couldn't yet name.

The house itself, with its tall bay windows and steep roof, was impressive enough. But the vast, wide-open space surrounding the building was breathtaking. A person could look out any given window and see nothing but nature, Lydia surmised. She had a feeling Chloe was going to love it here.

The rest of the afternoon Lydia spent getting acquainted with her family and her new surroundings. She toured the house, got familiar with the rooms she, Chloe, and Mrs. Porter would occupy, and looked at photo albums. She learned she had once taken ballet, voice, and violin lessons, and she wondered if she would still be able to dance, sing, or play the violin if she tried.

A stark reminder of what had been taken from her came when Jennifer pulled out Lydia's scrapbook of wedding plans. Everything had been organized with precision—bridesmaids' dresses, groomsmen's tuxedos, types of flowers—right down to how much each item would cost. The prices astounded Lydia.

How did I do it? she wondered. She could put a house in order faster than Mr. Clean, but thoughts of keeping books and organizing big events terrified her. From the looks of her wedding planner, her wedding was to have been a *big* event.

The final page included the wedding announcement that had been published in the local newspaper. She and Daniel had planned to marry in the First Community Church of Quinn Island, because, Jennifer said, it was the only local church big enough for the wedding party and anticipated crowd. Then, after a Paris honeymoon, they were going to live in Daniel's house while they built another.

Lydia closed the planner with a dismal sigh. What a charmed life she must have led. Too bad she couldn't remember any of it.

Daniel's parents arrived for supper. His father was also an attorney and shared his partnership with his son. Mrs. Matthews worked diligently in the Quinn Island Historical Society, the woman's club, and an organization that housed foster children until suitable homes could be found. They both greeted Lydia in a way that made her feel just as loved as her own parents had, then oohed and ahhed over Chloe like true doting grandparents.

Time passed. Mr. and Mrs. Matthews left. Chloe, who had missed her afternoon nap, and Mrs. Porter, who'd also missed hers, wore down and went to bed. Then a somnolent quietness fell over the five remaining adults, as though they were all tired and weary, with nothing noteworthy left to say. Eventually, Bill and Margaret retired, and Jennifer soon followed;

she rented a town apartment, but she had decided to spend the night at her parents' home in celebration of Lydia's return.

Daniel remained until shortly before midnight, then stood from where he sat next to Lydia on the sofa and held out his hand. "Walk me out?"

When they stepped out onto the wide front porch, she turned around to face him. He captured both of her hands in his, and for a moment he simply looked down at her. She wished she could see his eyes, read what was in them. But the overhead light threw dark shadows over the deeper planes of his handsome face, concealing whatever silent message he held there.

"I'm going to miss you tomorrow," he finally said.

A thump of fear hit Lydia in the chest. Her eyes stretched wide. "Miss me? You mean, I won't see you tomorrow?"

A pleased grin pulled at the corner of his mouth. "Do you want to?"

Realizing how childish she'd sounded, she ducked her head.

He released one of her hands and curled his forefinger beneath her chin, lifting her head so that she was again looking at him. "I want to see you, too, but I thought your parents and Jennifer would want to spend some time with you and Chloe tomorrow."

Of course, he was right. But thoughts of being away from him for the first time since meeting him three days ago triggered a strange and inexplicable uneasiness inside her. But what could she do about it? Fall down on her knees and beg him not to leave her alone at the mercies of her new and unfamiliar world?

She thought not.

"You're right," she said, forcing so much bravery into her voice, she sounded like an amateur actor in an unrehearsed play. "I do need to spend tomorrow with my family."

What about the next day? she wanted to ask. After all, it

was Saturday. Would he want to see her then? And why did she so desperately want him to want to?

"How about dinner tomorrow night?" He moved his hand from beneath her chin and brushed the backs of his fingers across her cheek. His gaze left hers and traveled over her face, like he was trying to carve her into his memory.

Her stomach fluttered. How was she supposed to focus on what he was saying when he touched her that way? "Dinner?" she finally managed to squeak.

He nodded. "We can call it the first official date of our new beginning."

"Okay," she agreed, her voice sounding small and faraway. Then her maternal instincts jabbed at her moonstruck conscience, reminding her she had one small priority. "What about Chloe?"

"I've already got that covered. She said she'd be ready at seven."

Lydia blinked. "You mean, you don't mind taking her along?" Jeff had often wanted to leave her behind.

He tugged on her hand, urging her to inch forward into his open arms. "Now, why would any man mind being the escort of the two most beautiful girls in the world?"

Lydia knew he was exaggerating, at least where she was concerned. But who was she to argue? He wanted to take Chloe along, and, whatever his reasons, that thrilled Lydia beyond description. She slipped her arms around his waist and rested her cheek against his chest. "Thank you, Daniel."

"For what?"

"For not leaving Chloe out."

"I like having her around."

Lydia closed her eyes. *So far, so good,* she thought with a contented sigh. *So far, so good.*

seven

The next morning, Lydia stood on the sidewalk outside Lydia's Boutique, perusing the dress shop with her mother, her sister, her daughter, and Mrs. Porter. When Margaret had asked Lydia what she wanted to do that day, Lydia had told her mother she'd like to see the shop. She was curious to see the place that was once so much a part of her life, see if she could envision herself working there. So far, she couldn't.

"It's hard to believe I actually own this place," she mused out loud.

"Trust me, you do," her mother said. "Jennifer has done a wonderful job keeping it open and profitable while you've been away, but it was your dream."

Lydia squinted through the bright morning sun as she studied the calligraphic lettering on the windowpane and the decorative trim on the eve spanning the front of the white frame building. Then she scanned her mother's and sister's faces, noticing their proud expressions. *Whose dream is it now?* she had to wonder.

She couldn't picture it as hers. In fact, she didn't think she had much fashion sense at all. She wasn't even fond of shopping. Of course, her life in Chicago hadn't offered her the opportunity to shop often. When she did, her purchases were always based on affordability.

Mrs. Porter had surprised her sometimes with an outfit beyond her own means, usually on a birthday or Christmas. But, generally, once Lydia got back on her feet after her long trek to recovery, her friend and former landlady had respected her desire to provide for herself and daughter.

Lydia noticed Margaret leaning heavily on her cane, and

she took the weary woman's arm. "Let's go inside so you can rest a little while."

Margaret gave her daughter a grateful smile, and the four women and Chloe went through the door.

Lydia had learned her mother's limp was a result of the surgery she'd had prior to Lydia's disappearance. Margaret had never fully recovered from the hip replacement, and Lydia couldn't help wondering what part grief over her abduction had played in her mother's incomplete recovery.

As she helped her mother negotiate the steps, a sad and discouraging thought filtered through her. She would never be able to replace all that was taken away that fateful night on a deserted highway. But she would do her best. She owed this woman, her sister, her father, and Daniel that much.

When Lydia stepped into the shop, she stepped out of her comfort zone. She glanced around in awe at rows and rows of stylish clothing, both women's and children's, hanging from wall racks and circular supports placed expertly across a polished hardwood floor. Lacy lingerie lined the shelves and supports at the back of the store. Two crystal chandeliers hung from a dazzlingly white ceiling, and soft classical music seemed to float through the walls. The two store clerks, one at the counter and one organizing a sales rack, both looked as though they had just stepped off the set of a classy New York fashion shoot.

Feeling a bit overwhelmed, Lydia drew in a deep breath, only to wish she hadn't. Even the air in the store smelled expensive.

"Mama, is this really your store?" Chloe asked, gaining her mother's attention.

Instinctively, Lydia lifted her daughter to her hip. She didn't want to be responsible for anything that might get broken by the curious four year old. "That's what they say, sweetheart."

"Can I have a new dress?"

"Of course you can, angel," a beaming Margaret answered.

"In fact, you can have all the new dresses you want."

"Maybe one," Lydia injected, intentionally keeping her gaze averted from her mother's. At some point, Lydia suspected she was going to have to talk to Margaret about who was mother to whom.

The salesclerk at the counter noticed the women and made her way to the front of the store, her gait reminding Lydia of a sleek, pampered house cat. "Hi, Jennifer," she said in a cultured voice that matched her cultured smile. "I thought you were taking the day off."

"I am. We just dropped by for a visit."

The two women engaged in what Lydia thought was an incomplete hug—they daintily grasped hands and merely touched cheeks together.

As they parted, the clerk, with her shiny black hair pulled back in a slick French chignon, fleetingly scanned each face as she turned to Margaret. Then her gaze snapped back to Lydia like a yo-yo on the rebound. After about two seconds of shocked paralysis, the elegant woman's painted mouth dropped open as though she'd just seen Lazarus raised from the dead.

Lydia forced herself not to withdraw. She figured she'd see many similar reactions in the next few days. She might as well start getting used to it.

Jennifer touched Lydia's arm. "Lydia, this is Jaime. She's the assistant manager of the store."

Lydia shifted Chloe to her left hip and extended her right hand. "Hi, Jaime. It's nice to meet you."

Jaime blinked like she'd been slapped. "Meet me? We went to school together. I was going to be in your wedding."

Lydia tried to muster up a smile but failed pitifully. "I'm sorry. I don't remember you. I have amnesia."

"Amnesia?" The clerk's voice rose and fell in a wave of shock.

"Yes." Lydia knew the woman deserved an explanation.

But Lydia wouldn't go into the details of her abduction in front of Chloe.

As though sensing her sister's distress, Jennifer shuffled toward the door and hooked her manicured hand in the crook of Jaime's arm. "Come in back with me for a minute. There's something I need to show you." With that, she led Jaime away.

Lydia breathed an inward sigh of relief, making a mental note to thank her younger sister later.

"Now," said Margaret, hobbling to a dress rack and flipping through the dresses there, "let's see what we can do about getting you started on a new wardrobe."

New wardrobe? Lydia blinked. She already had a wardrobe. She looked down at her ribbed pink shell, full-length denim skirt, and navy sandals. Of course, her closet wasn't stocked with stylish designer classics, like her mother and Jennifer wore. One couldn't find many of those in discount stores and thrift shops. But her meager collection served its purpose.

"Chloe and I really need only one dress each, to wear on our dinner date tonight with Daniel."

Her mother didn't seem to hear her.

Lydia sent Mrs. Porter a *what-should-I-do?* look. The older woman lifted her shoulders in a *don't-ask-me* gesture, then turned and started flipping through some dresses on a sale rack.

"What about this?" Margaret turned to display a red dress designed to mold a curvy body.

Lydia didn't think she had many curves to mold. Even if she did, they weren't for anyone's eyes but her own and, maybe someday, a husband's. She shook her head. "It isn't me."

Puzzlement pinched Margaret's forehead. "You don't like it?"

"It's okay. It's just not something I would wear."

"Why don't you try it on and then decide?"

Lydia held up a hand. "Really, there's no need."

An injured look fell over Margaret's face as she turned and

hung the dress back on the rack. She hobbled to a chair next to the dressing area and sat down.

Oh, great, Lydia thought. *Now I've hurt my mother's feelings.*

She set Chloe down and searched another rack, pulling out the first dress she came across in her size and style. Holding the garment up in front of her, she stepped up to her mother. "What do you think about this?"

Margaret critically eyed the dress, then lifted her gaze to her daughter's. "Do you want the truth, dear?"

The smile Lydia had pasted on for her mother's benefit wavered. "Of course."

"It doesn't suit you."

Well, touché, thought Lydia. She supposed one turn deserved another. Although she really hadn't meant to offend Margaret by rejecting the dress she'd chosen. Lydia was just stating a fact, her opinion, which, she'd noticed, didn't always set well with her mother.

"What are we looking for?" Jennifer asked, rejoining the group.

"Chloe and I need something to wear tonight. We have a dinner date with Daniel."

Jennifer's eyes lit up like a sunbeam. "Let me see what I can find." Like a kid on a treasure hunt, she scampered away and started digging through the racks.

Lydia's lips curved as she watched her sister retreat. Jennifer seemed so well suited for the affluent dress shop's environment. Much more so than Lydia herself did.

Margaret spurned Lydia's invitation to join her and Jennifer in their search, claiming she needed a while longer to rest her leg. So Lydia left the pouting woman and returned the dress she held to the rack. As she reached to hang up the garment, she caught a glimpse of the price tag and realized her mistake. The one hundred dollars she had removed from her savings pouch and tucked into her billfold before leaving the house was barely enough to buy Chloe an outfit, much less purchase one for herself.

She turned to Jennifer and Mrs. Porter, who both seemed intent on finding her the perfect garment for her evening out with Daniel. "You know what?" she said. "I think I may have something to wear back at the house, after all. Why don't we just concentrate on finding something for Chloe today?"

"Oh, come on, sis," Jennifer said, inspecting a short, black, sequined dress that sparkled like a blanket of black diamonds under the chandeliers. "What's one more outfit?"

About two hundred bucks, Lydia was tempted to say, but she decided to keep the quick retort to herself. Aloud she said, "One more than I really need."

Jennifer gave Lydia a baffled look. "That never stopped you before."

Lydia sent the baffled look right back. "It didn't?"

"Of course not." Jennifer held the dress up to Lydia. "Your philosophy was always that a woman couldn't have too many clothes. Your closet was the envy of every female in Quinn Island."

Perplexity creased Lydia's forehead. She knew Jennifer hadn't meant to be critical. She'd simply blurted out a statement of fact from one sister to another. Still, Lydia couldn't help feeling a little offended. She was also a bit unsettled by what this particular revelation about herself revealed. Had she really been so self-absorbed and frivolous with her money when so many people in the world were cold, hungry, and homeless?

Still trying to digest the information, she looked down at the dress Jennifer held up before her. Embarrassment crept up her neck just looking at the garment. She had T-shirts that were longer.

"Where are my old clothes?" she asked, figuring she might find something among her pre-amnesia wardrobe to wear for her date.

"We had everything put into storage when the lease on your apartment ran out. All that stuff is at least five years old. Why don't you try this on? I think it'll look great on you."

As gently as possible, Lydia pushed the dress away. "I don't think so. But, thanks, anyway."

Mrs. Porter, who'd been flipping through the sale rack all along, turned with a knowing grin and held up a dress that halted Lydia's ready protest. The younger woman stood dazed for a moment, admiring the sleeveless garment with its modest scooped cowl neck, trim waistline, and long skirt that graced yards and yards of silky beige material she knew would feel like luxury floating around her ankles.

She reached out and turned over the tag. Just as she feared. Even with the discount, she didn't have enough to buy a dress for both her and Chloe. And Chloe's needs came first.

She dropped the tag, brushing her fingers across the smooth material as she pulled her hand away. "It's a lovely dress, Mrs. Porter. But, really, I'd rather concentrate on getting Chloe one today."

Jennifer touched Lydia's arm. "Liddi, what is it?"

"Nothing," she answered, feeling the weight of her sister's perusal bearing down on her.

"Is it money you're worried about?"

"No," she lied. "I just didn't bring enough along today to pay for two dresses. I'll get Chloe one today, and come back and get mine later."

Understanding curved Jennifer's lips. "Lydia, that isn't necessary."

"Of course it is."

"Lydia," Mrs. Porter spoke up, "I think what your sister is trying to say is that you own the shop. The dresses won't cost you anything."

But Lydia had already thought about that. She gave the dress a palms-out gesture. "That dress cost this shop something. It's not right for me to just take it."

"Lydia—" Jennifer started, then stopped and rubbed her fingertips across her forehead, as though she were having second thoughts about what she'd intended to say.

"What?"

The younger sibling shook her head. "Nothing." She turned and motioned to Jaime, then reached for the dress in Mrs. Porter's hand. As the clerk stepped up to them, Jennifer said, "Jaime, go figure our cost on this dress and let me know what it is, please."

Jaime nodded and walked away. When the clerk was out of earshot, Jennifer turned back to Lydia. "Lydia, you have money. Since Daniel's the family attorney, we turned your finances over to him to take care of while you were away. I'm sure he'll go over everything with you when he has a chance." She squeezed Lydia's hand. "I just thought you'd want to know that."

Jennifer knelt in front of Chloe. "Now, let's go see what we can find you to wear, princess, while your mother tries on her dress."

Margaret decided she wanted to be a part of finding her granddaughter a frock. With the enthusiasm of two fairy godmothers contemplating a peasant maiden's costume for a ball, she and Mrs. Porter followed Jennifer and Chloe to the children's section of the shop, leaving Lydia to try on her dress alone. And to think.

So, I have money, she mused as she stepped into a fitting room. How much money? Enough to buy her and Chloe a small place of their own? Enough to help fund the new homeless shelter for which Jeff was trying to raise money? What about the missing persons' organization her mother had founded in her honor? Would a few extra funds help find another lost loved one?

She unzipped the dress and slid it from its hanger. What would it feel like having enough money to grocery shop without having to check the prices of every item on her list?

Put more than a widow's mite in the offering plate on Sunday? Buy Chloe that one special dress?

Mentally, she pulled back the reins of her elaborate thoughts and slipped the dress over her head. She'd better wait and talk to Daniel about her net worth before making plans to build houses or fund homeless shelters.

As she twirled in front of the mirror, inspecting the most beautiful garment she ever remembered seeing, her thoughts turned to her and Chloe's dinner date with Daniel. With very little deliberation, she decided to buy the dress.

Chloe chose a purple frock with a high waistline and white lace trim, which didn't surprise Lydia. Purple was her daughter's favorite color.

With the outfits hanging from fancy silk-covered hangers and protected with long garment bags bearing the store emblem, Lydia left the shop with just over fifteen dollars in her purse. Hopefully, the White Seagull, her sister's restaurant of choice for lunch, would be easy on the pocket.

Fortunately, it was. Lydia breathed a sigh of relief as she glanced at the menu posted outside the café entrance. The quaint little establishment had outdoor seating with a view of the marsh channel that separated the island from the mainland. The table umbrellas flapped occasionally in a breeze brisk enough to offer comfort to the patrons but tame enough that it didn't send the eating utensils flying.

As soon as they all settled around the table, Margaret leaned on her forearms and looked at Lydia. "Sweetheart, why don't I call Judy Spivey, your old hairdresser, and see if she can work you and Chloe in this afternoon?"

The question—which sounded more like the follow-up statement to a decision that had already been made—caught Lydia off guard. She couldn't think of an immediate response.

"She always did such a good job with your hair before," her mother added. "And don't you think Chloe's hair would look better in a chin-length bob?"

Self-consciously, Lydia raised a hand to her thick, wind-tossed tresses. She was rather fond of her hair just the way it was, even if her corkscrew curls did usually have a stubborn will of their own. As for Chloe, well, she'd been a bald new-born and a fuzzy toddler. It had taken four years for her hair to reach shoulder length. No way was anyone going to lay scissors to those light blond locks just yet.

Silently praying she wouldn't offend her mother again, Lydia reached over and covered the woman's hand with her own. "Give us a few days to get settled in, then we'll see about making an appointment with the hairdresser."

"But what about your date tonight?"

Lydia squeezed her mother's hand. "We'll get by," she said with an appeasing smile, then gratefully reached for the menu the waitress had just laid on the table.

Thankfully, Margaret let the matter drop, but Lydia had a feeling it would be picked up again later.

Lydia had helped Chloe with the child's menu and was trying to decide between the homemade vegetable soup and the chef's salad for herself when she heard Chloe giggle. Curious, Lydia cut her daughter a sidelong glance to find the child cupping a hand over her mouth, trying to stifle laughter. Lydia shifted her gaze to the other women at the table. They were all looking at her with amusement in their expressions, like some sort of conspiracy was under way.

Then everything turned black.

eight

Smiling, Lydia raised her hands to the fingers covering her eyes. She'd known those hands only four days, but would recognize them anywhere—even if she went another five years without feeling their touch.

An unexpected yearning wove through her, and for the first time since seeing her face on *Without a Trace*, she felt grievously cheated. Half a decade ago, she had not only been robbed of her past life, but of her precious memories of Daniel.

She pulled his hands away from her eyes and twisted her head around, looking up into his handsome face. His muscular forearms were exposed by dress shirtsleeves rolled up to his elbows, and beneath the unbuttoned top button of his shirt, his tie hung loose like he'd pulled at the knot with his forefinger. The wind pushed his dark hair flat against his forehead. His smell, all man heightened by a faint scent of spicy cologne, wrapped around her senses like a silk thread.

He captured one of her hands before she could drop it back to the table. "Fancy meeting you here," he said. "I knew there was a reason I was craving one of the Gull's subs today. My guardian angel was sitting on my shoulder, pointing me in your direction."

He leaned down and kissed her forehead, and Lydia released an inward sigh of contentment. He seemed to know just what to say and do to make her feel cherished.

Before letting go of her hand, he gave her fingers a gentle squeeze. Then he turned to Chloe, lifting the eager four-year-old out of her chair and up over his head. "And what about you, angel face? Have you been keeping these ladies straight?"

Chloe's answer was an attack of giggles.

A stranger looking on would think he had made the move a thousand times. Was he this way with all kids? Or did he see something special in Chloe?

Or was Lydia engaging in wishful thinking?

"Me and Mama bought pretty dresses for our date with you tonight," Chloe said as Daniel lowered her to his hip.

Daniel flashed Lydia a pleased smile, then turned his attention back to Chloe. "You did?"

"Uh-huh." Chloe gave her head an emphatic nod. "Mine's purple."

"Purple? I like purple. You'll make all the other girls very jealous."

He tickled Chloe's stomach, sending her off in another fit of giggles, before setting her back in her seat.

"Why don't you join us, Daniel?" Margaret suggested.

"I believe I will. Let me go wash up and I'll be right back." With that, he headed for the indoor area of the restaurant.

Lydia returned to her menu and had just about decided on the soup when a hand holding a small tape recorder appeared in front of her face, blocking her view.

"Miss Quinn," an unfamiliar male voice said, "could you answer a few questions about your abduction and the five years you were away from Quinn Island?"

She tipped up her head and looked into the eager face of a young man in a crumpled gray suit with press credentials clipped to the jacket pocket. A thirty-five millimeter camera dangled around his neck, and the end of his tie lay across the top of his shoulder, like he'd been running.

Lydia blinked. "I. . .ah. . ." Words failed her. She stared up at the man, unable to react.

"I understand you have a young daughter. Is this her? Is she a result of the assault, or do you know who the father is?"

Seconds passed like long minutes. Lydia became aware that everyone in the busy eating area was staring at her. The invisible walls of the outdoor café started closing in on her, trapping her. Still, she couldn't react, couldn't speak.

Out of the corner of her eye, she saw her mother and Mrs. Porter start to rise; then, for some reason, both ladies sat back down.

That "some reason" appeared instantly at her side in the form of Daniel. He clamped his hand over the microphone end of the recorder. "No, Mark, Miss Quinn will not answer any questions."

The man swung toward Daniel. "As a member of the media, I've got rights—"

"So has Miss Quinn." Daniel's voice was calm.

"But—"

"I can go talk to the judge." Daniel's tone remained low and steady, but Lydia could see a vein throbbing beneath his ear, and she sensed the fury caged just beneath the surface of his dark eyes. "I'm sure he'll have no problem issuing a restraining order to anyone who comes within a hundred feet of Miss Quinn with the intention of invading her privacy."

Lydia thought surely the reporter would back down. Amazingly, the smaller man persisted. "Come on, Daniel. The people of Quinn Island have a right to hear her story."

Daniel pulled his hand away from the tape recorder. "Then there's always harassment. Did you get that on record, Mark?"

The reporter snapped off the recorder and crammed it in his jacket pocket. "I'll get my story," he sneered. "I have another source, you know." With that, the irate man turned and stalked away.

Lydia propped her elbows on the table, dropped her forehead to her hands, and started shaking.

Daniel slid a chair against hers and sat down, slipping his arm around her shoulders. "Lydia, are you okay?"

The words on the menu blurred. Her world tilted. Someone touched her arm.

"Lydia," came her mother's concerned voice, "can I get you something? A glass of water?"

She heard everyone calling to her, but the darkness closing in around her was stronger. She couldn't pull herself back from it. The menu started to fade.

"Mommy!"

That did it. The alarm in Chloe's voice jerked her up straight. She focused on her child, and the concern and confusion in her small face bruised Lydia's heart. "Mommy's fine, sweetheart." They reached for each other at the same time. Lydia shifted her daughter to her lap. With arms and legs, Chloe clamped onto her mother's neck and waist and laid her head on her mother's shoulder.

"Did that man hurt you?" the little girl wanted to know.

"No, sweetie. He didn't hurt me."

"Then why did Daniel make him go away?"

In her peripheral vision, Lydia saw Daniel open his mouth to answer. She held up a hand to stop him. When she felt assured of his silence, she took the same hand and rubbed her daughter's back. "Because the man was asking about things I didn't want to talk about."

"What kind of things?"

Lydia pursed her lips, thinking. "Private things."

"Like my private places, where no one's s'pose to touch me."

"Yes. Something like that." Lydia felt her face warm, but she was awed by how closely her daughter's comparison paralleled her own feelings. Chloe was a private part of Lydia she had always been able to protect from evil and harmful things. At least, she had until today.

Chloe planted her small hands on her mother's shoulders and pushed back. "We need to pray for him." She bobbed her head with each word for emphasis. "Like Moses prayed for his people."

Lydia tucked a wisp of stray hair behind her daughter's ear. "You're right. We should." But she wasn't quite ready to forgive the stranger who had so rudely intruded on her and her daughter's life.

The waitress appeared at the table and Lydia asked Chloe if she was ready to order.

Wrinkling her nose, the little girl shook her head. "I'm not hungry anymore."

"Me, either." Lydia glanced around the table. "I think Chloe and I will just wait in the car."

Daniel stood, reaching for the back of her chair. "Come on. I'll take you back to the house."

She looked up at him. "But don't you have to get back to the office? And what about lunch?"

"We'll fix us something there." He captured her upper arm and helped her stand.

"But I don't want to be an imposition."

He trapped her chin beneath his thumb and curled forefinger. "You, my dear, could never be an imposition."

Lydia had no more energy to argue. She turned to her longtime friend. "Mrs. Porter—"

Mrs. Porter waved a hand through the air, shooing Lydia, Chloe, and Daniel away. "You run along, dear. I'll come with Margaret and Jennifer."

With Chloe perched on her hip, Lydia left the restaurant under the security of Daniel's protective arm. But inside she felt like she was dangling from a faulty trapeze swing with no safety net beneath her. What had just happened back there with that reporter? When he had asked about Chloe, she couldn't move, couldn't speak, couldn't react. All she could do was sit there and stare at him.

Then there was Daniel, like her own guardian angel, putting the reporter in his place, taking care of her. . .and Chloe. What would she have done today if he hadn't been there?

Daniel took the initiative and fastened Chloe's seat belt, then opened the door for Lydia. She climbed in like a battery-operated doll with a weak battery. As she watched Daniel circle the front of the car on his way to the driver's side, the layers of numbness began to peel away from her brain, leaving her mind exposed to the stark reality of her situation.

She needed him.

She felt a crack in her wall of independence, a small piece chip away. She needed Daniel, but God knew she didn't want to.

Ever since the day she had recovered from the assault and started making her own way, she had been determined not to need anyone. Not Jeff. Not even Mrs. Porter.

Not anyone.

Because she knew too well that fate could deal a person a cruel blow—and he or she could find themselves alone, like she had five years ago. During her recovery—when someone else had held the soupspoon to her mouth, bore her weight every time she went to the bathroom, provided her with a roof over her head—she had discovered that dependence was not the kind of existence she wanted for herself. And when she rose above it, she vowed she'd never go back.

She might one day fall in love with Daniel, marry him, share his home and children. But she *did not* want to depend on him for survival. Because if she did, and then something happened one day to take him away from her, she feared she might curl up into a ball and die, like she'd tried to do before she had Chloe. She didn't want to risk going back to that terrible feeling of helplessness. She didn't want to care about anyone that much. But she had a sinking feeling it was too late—and an even deeper fear that her dependence on Daniel went beyond basic need. Far beyond.

He had stepped into her life, swept her off her feet, carried her over the rough places, and, so far, had refused to put her down. What would happen if he decided to? Would her heart survive it?

The leather seat of the car creaked a little under Daniel's weight, and he touched her face. She closed her eyes and tilted her head so that her cheek rested in his palm.

Heaven help her, she needed him.

❧

"What was the reporter talking about when he said he had another source of information on me?" Lydia asked while she and Daniel prepared two ham and cheese sandwiches. Chloe, who sat at the table engrossed in a coloring book and crayons, preferred plain cheese.

Since Friday was the maid's shopping day, Lydia, Daniel, and Chloe had the house to themselves during lunch, which suited Lydia just fine. Something about spreading her own mayonnaise and slicing her own tomatoes helped her corral her scattered nerves and made her feel more at home in the spotless plantation house kitchen.

"Mark dates Jaime," Daniel answered as he slapped two slices of ham on his sandwich. He started to follow suit with Lydia's, but she fanned away the second piece of meat with an inward shudder. Where did he put all the food he consumed? Certainly not on that lean, muscular frame of his.

She added the cheese. "You mean the clerk at the dress shop? The one who told me she was supposed to have had a part in our wedding?"

He added slices of tomato. "That's the one."

On went blankets of lettuce. "So, that's how he found out I was going to be at the White Seagull. We were talking about it at the shop when we checked out."

The top layer of bread fell into place. "I would say so."

The phone rang, and Lydia almost jumped out of her slippers. With one hand over her racing heart, she turned to pick up the wall receiver.

Daniel abandoned the glass he was filling with ice and grabbed her wrist. "Don't answer that."

She frowned up at him. "Why? It could be Jennifer or Mother. Or Mrs. Porter."

"Let me." He squeezed between her and the wall and

picked up the receiver. "Hello."

Almost immediately, he scowled. "No, Miss Quinn will not be available to answer any questions this evening." A short pause, then, "No, she won't be available tomorrow, either." His scowl deepened. "Not then, either. She's not interested in talking to the press, period." His hand, which still circled her wrist, inched down to grasp her hand. "Not that it's any of your business, but I'm her attorney, and, no, I'm not interested in talking to the press, either. Thank you, and have a good day."

With that, he hung up and turned to her. He raked his free hand through his hair. A rebellious lock dipped toward his left brow. "Lydia, I don't think it would be a good idea for you to answer the phone for the next few weeks."

She didn't have to guess at the meaning of his words. "Daniel, exactly how many people do you think know I'm back by now?"

He pursed his lips, glancing into the distance over her left shoulder as though mentally stacking numbers, "Oh"—he cut his gaze back to hers—"I'd say about half the town."

Chewing her lower lip, she pulled her hands from his and turned, taking a few steps away from him. "Goodness, news travels fast here, doesn't it?"

"News like this does."

His hands cupped her shoulders. Drawn by his magnetic touch, she leaned back into him. His strong, comforting arms enveloped her shoulders. She raised her hands to his forearms and laid her head back against his chest. He rested his chin on top of her head and, ever-so-gently, began to sway from side to side. She closed her eyes and floated with him, feeling as though they moved as one, like ice dancers skating to a love song.

"I know your amnesia puts you at a disadvantage, love," he said. "Everyone here knows you. You don't remember anyone. But we'll get through this together, you and I."

She released a rueful sigh. "Seems like, Mr. Matthews, I've become somewhat a burden for you."

"On the contrary, Miss Quinn. You've given me back my reason for living."

A hand came up and brushed the hair away from her temple. His soft lips touched the jagged scar there. She felt the sting of tears behind her closed eyelids, and an overwhelming need to say "I love you." But the words tripped over the lump of emotion lodged in her throat.

He slid his palms up her arms, stopping when he reached her shoulders. Slowly, he turned her around. She knew he was going to kiss her and that she was going to kiss him back. A dizzy current raced through her as she floated toward him.

But ten small fingers crawling up her leg shattered her cloud of ecstasy in a million tiny pieces.

She pushed away from Daniel and looked down. What on earth had she been thinking? A trembling hand rose to her fluttering stomach. Obviously, she hadn't been thinking. Otherwise, she wouldn't have forgotten her daughter was sitting at the table less than six feet away.

She kneeled down in front of Chloe and grasped her daughter's hands. "What is it, sweetheart?"

Chloe tilted her head to one side, pushed out her lower lip in an artful pout, and looked at her mother with eyes that reminded Lydia of a wounded puppy. "I want you to hold me, Mommy."

Chloe only used "Mommy" when she really needed, or just plain wanted, her mother's attention. This was one of those "just plain wanted" times. But Lydia couldn't fault the timing. Had it not been for her daughter's interruption, she would have been engaged in the kind of scene she censored when Chloe watched TV. Lydia even blushed when she saw a man and woman locked in a passionate kiss on the television screen. That kind of intimacy, in her opinion, belonged to the privacy of the two consenting adults. Anything more belonged within the sanctity of marriage.

"Now, Chloe," Lydia said, "I think you're big enough to walk. Besides, if I hold you, who's going to carry our food to the table?"

Chloe turned huge accusing eyes on Daniel.

In answer to her daughter's silent message, Lydia said, "I was hoping we could eat out on the terrace"—she really needed the fresh air—"and I don't think it's fair to ask Daniel to carry all the food out there by himself. Do you?"

Chloe ducked her head and shook it.

When Lydia stood, she noticed a look of sincere remorse on Daniel's face.

"I'm so—"

She cut off his apology with an upheld hand. "It wasn't your fault." Scooping up hers and Chloe's plates, she headed for the terrace, knowing without looking that her daughter followed close behind.

"I'll be out in a minute," she heard Daniel say, but she never looked back, never broke her stride.

She didn't blame him for their momentary loss of self-control. He was a man. A passionate man who had, from day one, been honest and open about his feelings for her. She, on the other hand, was the mother of an impressionable four-year-old who had been sitting right there in the kitchen with her and Daniel when she had so willingly fell into his arms.

How could she have been so stupid?

❧

How could he have been so stupid?

Daniel berated himself while he stood, hands stuffed in his pockets, watching the two most important people in his life disappear through the kitchen door. In a moment of passion, he'd forgotten all about Chloe—and his vow to let Lydia make the first move.

She was so vulnerable right now, trying to find her place in a world she knew nothing about, live among people who unknowingly placed high demands on her. He didn't want to be one of those people. In fact, "those people," as well meaning as some might be, were exactly what he wanted to protect her from. Now, here he had gone and almost given in to his increasing desire to hold and kiss her. He would have if Chloe hadn't intervened.

He leaned back against the cabinet and scrubbed a shaky hand down his face. He needed to get out to the terrace and figure out how to worm his way back into Chloe's good graces. But he couldn't. Not right this minute. His insides were still quivering.

&

Some two minutes later, when Daniel felt his emotions were under control, he carried his sandwich and the drinks—purple Kool-Aid per Chloe's request—outside on a tray. He cautiously sat down in the vacant seat next to Chloe, positioning himself on the side of the child that was opposite her mother.

The first five minutes, he got nowhere. He talked and asked questions he thought four-year-olds might be interested in answering. Chloe chewed on her plain cheese sandwich, sipped her purple drink, and pointedly ignored him. The heel of her tennis shoe tapped out a steady *thump, thump, thump* on the chair leg as she swung her short leg back and forth.

He looked to Lydia for help. She merely gazed back at him with a twinkle in her eyes, then glanced away and took a dainty sip of drink, trying, he could tell, not to laugh.

She was enjoying seeing him squirm. *Spiteful woman,* he thought with affection, then almost grinned himself. Guess it served him right for losing his head and crawling all over her in the kitchen in front of her daughter.

He heaved a sigh and went back to Chloe. He'd interrogated hard-core criminals who had been easier to crack than this kid. "You know what, Chloe? I know where there's an ice cream parlor that serves purple ice cream."

Her leg stopped swinging. She stopped chewing.

Daniel waited a few seconds, then added, "Do you like purple ice cream?"

One, two, three seconds passed before Chloe nodded, once, without looking at him, then went back to chewing. Her leg went back to swinging.

At last, they were getting somewhere. Daniel felt like raising his hands and physically praising the Lord.

After fifteen minutes and a promise of a purple ice cream cone the very next day, Daniel felt confident all was forgiven. Chloe was talking and smiling again at his corny jokes, and the untimely kitchen incident seemed to be fading quickly from her young mind.

At least he thought so until she twisted her head around, peered up at him, and said, "Are you going to marry my mama?"

Daniel blinked. Now, how was he supposed to answer that? He glanced at Lydia, who looked the other way. No help there.

He folded his arms on the table and looked down at Chloe. Wanting to stay on good terms with the child, he gave an answer he felt was both unassuming and honest. "Maybe. Someday."

"That's what she says about Jeff."

Lydia swung her head around, gaping at Chloe like the child had just revealed a well-guarded secret.

Daniel almost choked on the last bite he'd taken of his sandwich. "She. . .says. . .what. . .about Jeff?"

"Whenever I ask my mama if she's going to marry Jeff, she always says 'Maybe someday,' " The singsong innocence of Chloe's voice did nothing to calm the spasms inside Daniel's chest.

Seemingly oblivious to the earthquake about to explode in the man beside her, the child turned her attention back to the sandwich she held in one hand and took another bite.

Daniel lifted a sharp, questioning gaze to Lydia.

"I'll explain later," she said with a nonchalant shrug.

Had she lied to him in Chicago when she told him she and Jeff were just friends?

She started stacking plates on the tray, and he followed suit with the glasses. She could count on explaining about Jeff. *Soon.* Like, within the next hour. No way was he going to spend the rest of the day wondering how she felt about this other man. And if she had any intentions of "maybe someday" marrying him, Daniel would simply have to change her way of thinking.

Because he had no intentions of her marrying anybody. . . except him.

nine

"I'm not sure going out tonight is such a good idea," Lydia told Daniel as she set the dishes in the sink.

Daniel understood her reservations, and he had already come up with a solution. Stepping up beside her, he slid his hands into his pockets so he wouldn't follow his instinct to touch her. "What if I were to take the afternoon off and take you and Chloe to a place where your privacy will be respected and no reporters will harass you?"

She shifted to face him. "I can't let you do that. You've already missed four days of work this week. You must have tons to do."

A sharp pang of regret jabbed at his chest. Once he had put his work before her, and his decision had cost them both—dearly. He would not make that mistake again.

"Only half a ton," he said, forcing a chipper note into his voice. "Which is nothing out of the ordinary. Besides, when I found you in Chicago on Tuesday, I went ahead and cancelled all my appointments for the week. The only thing waiting back at the office for me is a stack of paperwork, which isn't nearly as appealing as spending an afternoon on the island with you and Chloe."

Her eyes lit up with a childlike exuberance. "The island?"

He nodded.

Even as she shook her head, he could see her struggling to contain her enthusiasm. "Seriously, Daniel. I don't want you to feel you have to entertain us."

Chloe was back at the table engrossed in her coloring, but Daniel suspected she was keeping a keen eye on him and her mother. He resisted the urge to reach for Lydia's waist and risked capturing her hands instead. "The only reason I went into work this morning was because if I hadn't, I would have been on your parents' doorstep at dawn wanting to see you, and I really felt your family needed a little time with you."

A well of emotion still too raw to be contained rose in his chest, as did the conviction in his voice. "Lydia, I have waited for this day for so long that I live in fear I'll wake up and find it's all been just a dream." He squeezed her fingers. "There's nothing at work that can't wait until Monday. But there's something here I've wanted for five years. I'd like to spend every minute with you that I can. That is, if you have no objections."

"I don't," she responded, her voice sounding small and breathless. "We'd love to go to the island with you."

A small degree of satisfaction settled over Daniel. Maybe, just maybe, she was beginning to feel for him just a little of what he felt for her. "Great. Let me make a phone call, and in about thirty minutes, we'll be set to go."

"Do Chloe and I need to change?"

He considered Chloe's shorts and Lydia's casual skirt and top. "No. You're both perfect just the way you are."

He placed his call, making arrangements to borrow a car since his was too easily recognized. In addition to the vehicle, he requested hats and sunglasses for himself, Lydia, and Chloe so they could leave the grounds in disguise.

When he hung up the phone, he turned around and squared off to face Lydia, who stood about three feet away, her hands laced in front of her. For a fleeting moment, he lost sight of his purpose. Did she realize what a captivating picture she made, standing there mesmerizing him with those soft brown eyes of hers? Somehow, he didn't think so.

Mentally, he shook his head, reminding himself of his intention. "Now, I'm ready to hear about Jeff," he said.

She shrugged. "There really isn't much to tell."

"Then it shouldn't take you very long."

She glanced pointedly at Chloe, then looked back at him,

clearly expecting him to relent and wait until later to hear what she had to say about Jeff.

Daniel merely leaned back against the counter, crossed his arms and ankles, and waited.

She studied him a moment, apparently contemplating what to do, then rolled her eyes and threw up her hands in defeat. "Come on, Chloe. Let's go see what's on PBS."

Chloe shot Daniel a wary look, and at first he feared she'd refuse to go.

Lydia held out her hand. "Come on, Chloe," she repeated with a mild note of firmness. "Daniel and I need to talk about something, then we're going to ride out to the island with him and see the ocean."

Chloe lit up like a sunbeam. "We are?"

Daniel sauntered to the table "That's right. We might even round up a bucket so we can play in the sand."

The child jumped down from her chair and, ignoring her mother's hand, dove for Daniel, wrapping her arms around his knees.

He peeled her arms from his legs and kneeled down in front of her. When she reached around his neck and planted a butterfly kiss on his cheek, his chest tightened. The sting of unexpected tears nipped at his eyes. He quickly blinked them away. The little girl's charms were as potent as her mother's, but in a totally different way.

Chloe followed her mother out of the kitchen with a jaunty bounce in her step and her ponytail swinging from side to side behind her. As soon as the door closed behind them, Daniel placed another quick call, adding a sand bucket, shovel, and a beach blanket to his earlier request.

When he hung up, he leaned back against the counter once again and tried to prepare himself for Lydia's return. What would he do if she told him she was in love with Jeff and was thinking about marrying him? He forced a deep breath into his lungs. He wasn't sure what he'd do. But, if he were a betting person, he'd wager he'd lay down and die, right there on the spot.

When she stepped back through the door, every muscle in his body tensed like a rope engaged in a tug-o-war game.

She stopped about three feet in front of him and crossed her arms. "You're buying her affection, you know."

One corner of his mouth tipped. "It's worth it."

Their eyes locked, igniting a bolt of electricity that crackled over several seconds of silence. Then she blinked, and he felt her pull herself back, as though she'd suddenly realized she was standing too close to a cliff ledge.

Shifting her weight to one foot, she said, "So, you want to know about Jeff."

He nodded, once. That was all the knot in his throat would allow.

"About two months ago he asked me to marry him."

He slowly arched an inquisitive brow. "And you were considering it?"

"I was. . .waiting."

"Waiting for what?"

"To see if something more than friendship would develop between us, or if a parental bond would develop between him and Chloe."

"And was anything developing?"

A soft smile curved her lips. "No. I realize now that Jeff and I are simply good friends. That's all we'll ever be. He knows that, too."

He heaved a deep sigh of relief. When he exhaled, his muscles turned to pulp as the tension drained from his body. He scrubbed a hand down his face. "I lost you once. I don't want to lose you again. To anything, or anybody."

They both grew still and very quiet, and Daniel saw a tenderness in her eyes he knew he'd never seen before. And in that single defining moment, he realized she cared about him. *Really* cared about him. About his thoughts, his feelings, and what he had suffered. Even after all she'd been through, she still found room in her heart to care about what her disappearance five years ago had done to him.

He was overcome with. . .something. He wasn't sure what. It was a feeling he'd never, until that moment, experienced. But whatever it was, it moved him. And humbled him.

"I was going to tell you about Jeff's proposal," she said, answering a question he'd asked himself at least a dozen times since Chloe had made her little earth-jarring statement a while ago. "Yesterday, before we left for the airport, I started to tell you, but the shuttle arrived and there wasn't enough time. Since then, I really haven't thought about it."

Daniel nodded, satisfied he knew all he needed to know. There was no one else, and she had planned to tell him about the proposal.

He eased away from the counter. "You know," he said, "I'd really like to hug you before we go, but I'm afraid to." Afraid Chloe would walk in. Afraid he couldn't let go.

Suddenly, she had the brown eyes of a minx and the mischievous grin of an imp. Strolling forward, she raised her hands to his waist. His throat went a little dry.

"Just don't forget my daughter's in the very next room," she said.

Daniel would have laughed out loud, but he didn't want to draw the protective four year old's attention just yet. Slipping his arms around Lydia, he said, "I think, *maybe,* I can manage that."

Her arms circled his waist and she laid her cheek against his chest. Feeling more contented than he had in a very long time, he rested his jaw on top of her head. My but she was full of surprise. Why hadn't he ever noticed that about her before?

❧

"Mama, are we goin' in that?" Chloe said from where she stood on the top step next to her mother.

The old SUV sitting in the circular drive had an unpainted front fender and a creased back bumper. Under a multitude of dings, dents, and scratches, lay a dull coat of yellow paint. Daniel had borrowed the eccentric-looking vehicle from his eccentric-looking cousin named Steve.

Pasting on a bright smile, Lydia peered down at her child, who now wore a floppy straw hat and a child-size pair of oval-lens sunglasses. "We sure are, honey. Wasn't it nice of Steve to let us borrow it?"

Chloe scrutinized the vehicle, but she made no further comment. She might not have been showered with many luxuries outside their basic needs, but she was accustomed to riding in Mrs. Porter's and now Daniel's comfortable, well-kept sedans.

Lydia donned her straw hat and sunglasses, and Daniel jammed a white baseball cap, bill turned backward, over his dark hair. He had also changed clothes and now wore an olive-green polo shirt, a pair of faded jeans, and a well-worn pair of running shoes.

He fastened Chloe in her seat and opened the door for Lydia. Amazingly, the inside of the car was as neat and clean as a king's castle and smelled as fresh as the morning sunshine. When Daniel fired the engine, it purred like a well-fed kitten.

Steve had left in Daniel's car about five minutes earlier, hoping to draw away any media or overzealous well-wishers who might be stationed at the front gate. Even so, as Daniel approached the entrance to the drive, unease stirred up a swarm of butterflies in Lydia's stomach. When the gate clanged shut behind them, she felt as though she'd been locked out of her house in the middle of a cold, dark night.

"Are you sure no one will bother us on the island?" she asked as Daniel eased out onto the highway.

He'd noticed how the knuckles of her clasped hands had turned white when he drove through the gate. Reaching over, he pried her hands apart and laced his fingers through hers. Her fingertips felt like icicles pressed against the back of his hand, but he wasn't surprised. Her hands had always gotten cold when she was nervous. Today, they had been cold a lot.

"If anyone sees you and recognizes you," he explained, "they may stop and say hello and tell you they're glad you made it home, but they won't bother you. Not like the people on the mainland who know you so well."

"Oh, Daniel, the people haven't bothered me so much, other than that nosy reporter." The last phrase she added as though she'd just tasted something sour. "It's just that everyone seems so thrilled to see me. Since I can't remember any of them, I can't empathize with their experience, because mine's a totally different one." She shook her head and turned her attention to the view outside the passenger window. "I don't mean to sound cold, but it's just going to take some time to recapture what I once felt for everyone."

Just like it'll take time to recapture what you once felt for me, Daniel thought. Something heavy settled on his chest. He shifted gears in the old five-speed. "You don't sound *cold*, sweetheart. I know it's going to take time."

And when she learned that five years ago a self-serving decision on his part had ultimately put her in the situation she was now in, would she even want to love him at all?

ten

Fifteen minutes later, Daniel drove over the bridge spanning the channel that separated the island from the mainland. About a quarter-mile after crossing the bridge, he veered to the right and drove down a street lined with sparse houses shrouded by verdant trees and lush landscaping.

Lydia eyed each home on the island with curiosity, noticing they were all modestly built, but well-kept and welcoming. When Daniel passed the first four without stopping, she said, "Which one belonged to my grandfather?" She simply couldn't see herself as the owner of one of these charming little cottages by the sea.

"You'll see," was Daniel's answer.

They passed a female jogger accompanied by a gorgeous collie on a leash. The runner gave the SUV a critical glower, but she showed no interest in the occupants.

A smile settled on Lydia's lips. So that was why Daniel had chosen such a deprived-looking vehicle for their outing. Onlookers paid more attention to the automobile than to who was inside.

"Mama, where's the ocean?"

Smiling, Lydia peeked around the bucket seat at her daughter, then looked to Daniel for the answer.

"It's on the other side of the houses, Chloe," he explained. "All those plants and trees around and between the houses were placed there on purpose, to make a shield between the road and the ocean."

"But when do *we* get to see it?" Chloe persisted.

He glanced at Chloe via the rearview mirror. "Soon, angel. We're just about there."

A kneeling elderly woman tending her flower bed raised her garden trowel in greeting. Returning the affable gesture, Lydia asked, "Are the people who live on the island friendly?"

"Very. They keep an eye out for one another, occasionally get together for things like barbeques and birthday parties. At the same time, they respect each other's privacy."

The small, wood-frame island church, supported by partially submerged stone pillars, appeared to be floating on top of the marsh. Daniel had told her the aged building had encountered at least a dozen major storms since it had been built over 120 years ago. Somehow, the old house of worship had withstood them all and was still standing.

As they drove past the church, Lydia decided Daniel was right when he had told her the island was like a world within itself. Strictly residential, no nightclubs, no bars, no social clubs that labeled one class or another. Just a safe haven for people who wanted to escape the madness of a harsh, demanding world and live in quiet tranquility.

A place for people like her. . .and Chloe.

The tension tugging at Lydia's nape began to ebb, heightening her awareness of Daniel's thumb caressing the back of her hand.

The road ended where someone's driveway began. Instead of stopping, Daniel pulled into the private road that was flanked on each side of the entrance by a replica of a ship's-helm wheel. He navigated a ninety-degree curve to the left and continued up a gently sloping hill, then stopped in front of a charming two-story cottage with a wraparound porch. The gray paint appeared fresh and unweathered, but the shrubs and flowers could have used the tender hand of a good gardener. The poor bushes either reached across the stone walkway like long, gnarly fingers or drooped in haggard disarray outside their intended boundaries. Lydia's hands itched to start pruning. The wide stone walkway that led up to matching front-porch steps added a pleasing touch of traditional grace and dignity to the quaint appeal of the structure.

Lydia studied the house and its surroundings with keen interest. It was the last building on the island, so there could be only one reason Daniel would stop here. "This. . .belongs to me?" Her disbelief spilled over into her voice.

"Yes. The cottage and the entire southern tip of the island is the property your grandfather left you seven years ago."

She shifted her gaze to his. She could tell from the expectancy in his expression he was waiting for her reaction.

So was she.

She studied the cottage once again. A lazy white cloud drifted behind the gabled wood-shingled roof. The sun, blazing high in the western sky, bathed the gray, trimmed-in-white house and its fertile surroundings in a soft blanket of white light, making it look almost ethereal. The fat leaves of two tall palm trees, one flanking each front corner of the house, swayed back and forth in a temperate breeze, as though beckoning her to step out of the car and come.

But something held her back. The excitement, thrill, and exhilaration she had expected to feel upon arriving at her island retreat had dwindled, leaving in their wake an odd sense of hesitation. How did she accept such a generous gift from someone long gone, someone she didn't even know?

A bump on her left elbow drew her attention. She swiveled her head around to find Chloe had unfastened her seat belt and scrambled to the space between the front bucket seats. Blue eyes wide, she gaped at the cottage "Is this our house, Mama?"

"Yes. I suppose it is." But it didn't seem real. In fact, nothing had seemed real since she left Chicago. Except Daniel. And, sometimes, she feared he was too good to be true.

"Are we gonna live here?" Chloe wanted to know.

"I don't know, honey. We'll just have to wait and see."

Lydia raised her eyes to Daniel's. The warmth in his smile

eased some of her trepidation.

"Would you like to have a look inside?" he asked.

"Isn't it locked?"

A grin curved his lips. "Yes, but I have a key."

One corner of her mouth quirked in amusement. "Why doesn't that surprise me?"

When she stepped out of the SUV, she drew in a deep breath. The balmy air smelled faintly of the flowering shrubs huddled around the house and something else. The salt and sea, maybe?

Lydia was anxious to see the beach. She wanted to see if the earth merging with an endless plane of water was really as awe-inspiring as she thought it would be, and to discover why the ocean had been so alluring to her in her second life—the one she'd lived as Sara.

"I'm sorry the yards have been neglected," Daniel said as they approached the stone front-porch steps. "The landscaper I was using moved away from Quinn Island. What with getting ready for the *Without a Trace* show and all, I haven't had a chance to replace him. I'll get on it first thing Monday, though."

"You'll do no such thing," Lydia said.

He stopped short on the second step, prompting her to glance back over her shoulder at him as she stepped onto the porch. He was staring at her with a strange, somewhat stunned, expression. She shifted around to face him. "What is it?"

"Why don't you want me to hire another landscaper?"

"Because I want to do it myself."

"Really, Lydia, it's no trouble. In fact, I already have one in mind."

"I'm not talking about hiring a landscaper, silly. I'm talking about doing the landscaping myself. I love yard work."

He blinked. "Are you serious?"

"Of course I am."

He continued staring at her as though she'd just dropped in from outer space.

"I have a feeling I just said something out of character here," she said.

He took the final two steps, forcing her to tilt her head in order to maintain eye contact. He stared down at her. "You used to hate yard work."

"I did?" She found that a little hard to believe.

"Yes, you did." He grasped her fingers and lifted her hand. Dropping his gaze to their point of contact, he added, "You didn't like messing up your hands." His thumb traced the irregular plane across her knuckles. "You have the most beautiful hands." A wistful smile tugged at the corner of his mouth. "You loved having your nails done."

She pulled her hand free of his and curled her fist in the folds of her skirt. Obviously, Daniel had taken a left turn down memory lane, because she didn't have beautiful hands anymore. While living in Chicago, she'd barely had time to file her nails once a week. She certainly hadn't had the time—or money—for something so frivolous as a professional manicure. And four years of cleaning had left her skin rough and dry despite the hand creams she used daily.

Still, given the choice of an hour at a manicurist's table and one planting and pruning the neglected foliage around the beach cottage, she'd choose the latter.

How would Daniel feel about that? Sorely disappointed, Lydia suspected.

"Mama, when we gonna get to see the water?"

"In just another minute or two," Daniel answered, pulling a set of keys from his pocket.

Grateful for the timely interruption, Lydia kneeled in front of her daughter. "I'm proud of you for being so patient, Chloe. Sometimes, when grown-ups get to talking, we get sidetracked."

"What's sidetracked?"

"It means sometimes we forget what we're supposed to be doing." It seemed she'd been doing that a lot over the past four days.

Daniel pushed the door open and stepped back. "Well, ladies, here we are."

Reaching for Chloe's hand, Lydia rose and stepped cautiously across the threshold. Entering the house felt eerie, like entering a vacated office building long after business hours. Her sandals echoed with a dull, hollow-sounding thud against the hardwood floor. White sheets draped over furniture cast ghostly impressions around the large, dusky room beyond the foyer. Dust fairies, awakened by human presence, danced in the sunlight that sliced through the open door behind them.

Chloe pressed her small body against her mother's thigh. Laying her hand on her daughter's shoulder, Lydia stopped short of stepping beyond the foyer. "It's okay, honey. Those are just bedsheets, spread over the furniture to keep it from getting dirty."

Daniel stepped up beside them, flipped a wall switch, and the bright overhead lights chased the spooky shadows into cheery pale yellow walls. A painting of a sailboat in a heavy gilded frame hung over what Lydia guessed was the living room sofa.

She noticed immediately the absence of cobwebs and dust buildup. The house might not have been lived in for seven years, but it certainly hadn't been neglected.

She cut Daniel a sidelong glance. "Let me guess. You've looked after this place for the last five years."

He shrugged. "I've tried. I have someone come in and clean occasionally, and I try to get out here once every month or so to see that everything's okay."

Scanning the room, she heaved a deep breath. "I don't know how I'm ever going to repay you for all you've done while I've been away."

He caught her chin between his thumb and forefinger, tilting her face toward his. "Love is free."

The room swayed, and Lydia wondered if a wave had slipped beneath the house and carried them out to sea.

"Mama, look."

Lydia hadn't even noticed that Chloe had left her side. A wing of panic fluttered in her chest when she didn't immediately see her daughter. Then she noticed the backs of two tiny pink tennis shoes planted beneath a child-shaped lump under the curtain hanging over the back door.

Daniel led Lydia across the room and pulled back the curtain. There stood Chloe, her little nose pressed against the full-length pane of a French door, a ring of fog where her breath fanned the glass. Beyond the window was the site Lydia felt she'd waited an entire lifetime—at least, the only life she could remember—to see. White crested waves rolled into shore, spreading a soft sheet of foam over bright pale sand, then languidly drifted back out to sea. A sailboat bobbed up and down amid a rippled blanket of diamonds tossed by the sun across the blue-green water. Two silver seagulls rode on the wind.

Both Chloe and Lydia gasped and jumped back when three large pelicans dipped in front of the door window.

"It's even more beautiful than I imagined," Lydia said.

Daniel reached around her and unlocked the door. "I'm glad you like it."

Like it? She had a feeling she was going to love it.

Daniel opened the door and the wind rushed in, catching her and Chloe both off guard as it pushed them backward. The breeze grabbed their hats and tossed them across the room at the same time Daniel reached out to support mother and daughter. His body was a sustaining wall that kept them from falling.

When Lydia and Chloe were both steady, Lydia said, "Wow, I never realized the wind would be so strong." Fortunately, she had pulled her hair back in a loose ponytail at the nape of her neck. She could just imagine what her stubborn curls would look like after an hour's tryst with this breeze.

"We're supposed to have some rain showers coming in this afternoon, so it's a little more brisk today than usual. Even so, it should be a little calmer down on the beach. Up here on the knoll, you get the full brunt of the breeze coming in off the ocean."

"Good, because I know a little girl who's going to be very disappointed if she can't at least get her feet wet." She knew a big girl who would be, too.

"Do you want me to get the stuff out of the car now or later?"

"Later," she said. Grasping his hand, she pulled him out the door behind her.

Hand in hand, with Chloe in the middle, they descended the stairway leading down to the sand. When they were two steps from the bottom, Lydia stopped, halting Chloe and Daniel in the process. "Is it okay if we take off our shoes?"

"Sure, if you want to."

She glanced down at Chloe, who peered back up at her through the sunglasses that were a small replica of her own. "What do you say, Chloe? Do we want to take our shoes off?"

"Will the beach hurt my feet?"

Daniel kneeled down next to Chloe. "No, sweetheart. The beach won't hurt your feet as long as you don't step on the sharp shells."

"Then we want to."

Side by side, she and Chloe sat down on the steps and removed their shoes, Chloe tucking her white socks neatly inside her sneakers before setting them next to her mother's sandals.

"Aren't you going to take yours off?" Lydia asked Daniel.

He took off his hat, turned it around so the bill was in its proper position, and jammed it back down on his head. "Maybe later."

She guessed he had his reasons. At the moment, she felt too happy and carefree to stand around and contemplate what they were. "Okay." She shrugged, then looked down at Chloe. "Ready?"

Chloe gave an emphatic nod.

Instead of taking off in an eager run, like she was tempted to do, Lydia took the first step slowly, relishing the feel of the warm, dry sand beneath her feet. She didn't want to miss a thing.

She took a few more steps, then crouched down, encouraging Chloe to squat next to her. Lydia scooped up a handful of the soft ivory earth and let the granules sift through her fingers. Chloe mimicked her mother.

Lydia watched her daughter concentrate on the sand leaving her small hand to be carried by the wind to another resting place a short distance away. "Doesn't that feel nice, Chloe?"

With all the seriousness of a scientist on the brink of a discovery, Chloe bobbed her head.

They rose and traveled the short distance to a ribbon of shells that had been washed ashore and deserted by the previous high tide. Lydia and Chloe knelt to examine the abandoned treasures, testing the shape and texture of several in their hands. Chloe chose two that particularly struck her fancy and shoved them into her shorts pocket, along with a handful of sand.

When they were satisfied they had, for the time being, viewed enough of the sea jewels, Daniel lifted Chloe over the crusty string of shells, then insisted on doing the same for Lydia.

Here, the sand was harder, cooler, packed by the countless waves that washed over it in the course of a day. Daniel bent down, slipped off his shoes and socks, and set them aside. When he straightened, Lydia quirked a quizzical brow.

He simply shrugged. " 'If you can't beat 'em. . .' "

Once again, they linked hands, this time with Lydia taking the middle position. It seemed appropriate, somehow, that she be linked to both her daughter and the man beside her—the man who had become such an integral part of her life in such a very short time—when she stepped out into the water for the very first time. Together, they walked to the line in the sand the last wave had made, then ambled a few steps further.

The next surge rolled in and surrounded their feet and ankles with a cold rush of water. Lydia and Chloe gasped. Chloe retreated a few inches, but made no effort to crawl up her mother's leg for protection, as Lydia had expected the child to do.

Then the wave rolled back out, and Lydia gasped again, instinctively tightening her hold on her daughter's hand. "Oh, my," she said. Something had slipped ashore and was pulling the sand out from under her feet.

In less than a heartbeat, Daniel's arm was around her. When the earth stopped shifting, she looked down to find a seemingly unperturbed Chloe watching the retreating water and grinning like she had just taken her first ride on a carousel and was awaiting her next. Had Lydia been the only one who had felt it?

She swiveled her head around and looked up at Daniel, whose face beamed with amusement. "I should have warned you," he said, without the slightest hint of remorse. "When the water goes out, it takes some of the sand with it. Makes you think the earth's opening up to swallow you."

She blinked. "Right. I suppose I should have figured that out." Somehow, the side of his shirt had gotten bunched up in her fist. She let go, cringing at the wrinkles she'd made.

Just as the next wave rolled in, Chloe pulled free. Lydia turned and started to reach for her daughter, but Daniel stopped Lydia with his hands on her waist.

"She's fine," he said.

Hesitantly, Lydia watched while Chloe started skipping in circles, giggling as the foamy water rolled in and swam around her feet, then eased back out to sea.

Lydia felt Daniel tug on her waist, urging her to lean back against him. A willing recipient of his support, she relented.

Once, Chloe glanced up at them and Lydia stiffened, remembering how her daughter had reacted the last time she was in Daniel's arms. But this time Chloe merely grinned at Lydia and Daniel, paying no mind to the cozy position they were in. "Look at me, Mama," she said. "I'm a mermaid." Then she went right on dancing with the sea, the sand, and the sun.

When Daniel chuckled, the muscles of his chest rippled across Lydia's back. After watching her daughter a long moment, a smile tipped Lydia's lips. She had never seen her usually reserved daughter so buoyant and deliriously happy. Lydia herself had never felt so buoyant and happy. So free.

Capturing the wind-tossed strand of hair that had escaped her ponytail, she looked out over the water. The sailboat was long gone, and now a fishing barge crawled across the horizon at a snail's pace. Overhead, in a sky-blue canopy blotted with clouds of cotton, a plane puttered by, towing a banner advertising where to get the cheapest beach towels and suntan lotion. Below, the cool water continued to tug around their ankles, shifting the sand beneath her feet.

Lydia rested her head back against Daniel's chest. He laid his jaw against her temple and started swaying from side to side in that steady, rhythmic way of his that made her feel they moved together as one. Closing her eyes, Lydia opened her heart and accepted the gift that her grandfather had so generously given. Contentment filtered in and filled a place inside her that for five long years had been empty. For the first time in her life that she could remember, she knew where she belonged.

eleven

Daniel laid Chloe on a freshly made bed in the cottage. Since the child was accustomed to an afternoon nap, she had worn down two hours into their beach excursion.

Instead of returning to the Quinns' so soon, Daniel had suggested they make one of the beds in the cottage for Chloe. He was thankful when Lydia agreed. Since their reunion, he hadn't had a chance to really talk to her, learn much about her life between Quinn Island and Chicago, simply be with her.

He pulled a thin cover up over Chloe's shoulders and kissed her soft, round cheek, lingering a few seconds. Beneath the sunscreen he'd insisted she and her mother apply while on the beach were several other refreshing scents: little girl, baby shampoo, and sunshine.

A longing so deep it hurt fisted inside Daniel's chest. In the short course of four days, he had come to realize he wanted to be this child's father. He wanted to be there to tuck her in every night, see her when she woke each morning, see her off on her first day of school, hear her excitement when she lost her first tooth. And he wanted to marry her mother. Wanted it so badly, his arms ached when he crawled into bed each night, alone.

What sometimes puzzled him, though, was that his feelings for Lydia seemed even stronger than they were before. How could that be?

He straightened the covers around Chloe's shoulders once more, even though they didn't need it. Maybe the old adage really did ring true. Maybe he simply hadn't known what he'd had until he'd lost it.

As he straightened, Lydia leaned over to kiss her daughter's cheek; then they crept from the bedroom and into the living room. He followed Lydia's lead as she wandered to one of the double windows overlooking the beach. Together, they opened the shutters. Dark, smoky-gray clouds were gathering on the horizon, and the waves breaking close to shore had grown more violent. The rain would be here soon.

Sliding his fists into his pockets, he shifted so that he faced her profile. In the silence that had fallen over the room, he watched as she stood, arms crossed, gazing out at the aggressive hands of Mother Nature.

He'd been doing that a lot today. Just watching her. At times, while they were on the beach, he'd wished he could see the world through her eyes. To her, every experience had been an adventure, every discovery a secret waiting to be revealed. Even though the light of eager excitement had shone in her lovely face as she canvassed the seashore, she had been a patient explorer, as though to hurry would be to miss something miraculous and spectacular. And her gentle endurance as she answered her daughter's one million and one questions had merely strengthened his growing need to become a father and a husband. Chloe's father. Lydia's husband.

His gaze slid to the view beyond the window. All ships and wildlife had run for cover in anticipation of the upcoming storm, leaving behind only the sand, the darkening sky, and the roiling waters. Daniel loved these waters. In fact, he jogged the island shores three times a week. Sometimes, more than that. Over the past five years, when the weight of the world, of losing Lydia, had become almost more than he could bear, he'd often found himself out there during the most desolate hours of the night. Something about feeling the damp, salt-laced wind whisper across his skin, watching the white-crested waves, like ghosts rising from the ocean, crash against the jetties, hearing the lone call of a night bird, left him with a sense of sanity he couldn't find anywhere else.

"Why me, Daniel?"

Lydia's soft voice penetrated his weighty thoughts. "Why you what?"

She angled her head and looked at him. "Why did my grandfather leave all this to me? Why not Jennifer, or my father?"

A smile of understanding tipped his lips. Her grandfather had once told him that when Lydia was a child, she would spend hours scavenging the beach with her grandmother, or digging up treasures in the sand, or simply watching the ocean. Even though that had changed as Lydia had gotten older, the late Otis Quinn had always felt she would one day return to the first place that had captured her heart—the island. That was why he'd left his beach cottage to her.

But Daniel knew that wasn't the answer she was looking for. "Your grandfather," he explained, "through inheritance and hard work of his own, obtained a substantial field of assets during his lifetime. Trust me, Lydia, everyone else got their fair share."

Shaking her head, she turned her attention back to the world beyond the window. "I wish he were here so I could thank him personally. This place feels like paradise to me."

"Me, too," he admitted.

A paradise that, five years ago, she had hated. The quiet seclusion, the boring neighbors, the remote solitude that Daniel found so calming. He studied her expression, fascinated at how she now looked at the capping waters through eyes of awe and wonderment. How long would it be before she remembered she wasn't interested in "living at the end of the earth"?

Daniel's last thought led to an even more perplexing question, one he was eager to have answered. "Lydia?"

"Hmm?" she muttered without looking at him, as though she were in a daydream and had no desire to leave.

"Will you ever regain your memory?"

She blinked, and that faraway expression of awe faded from her face. Slowly, she turned her head and looked at him with a mixture of trepidation and uncertainty, like a novice swimmer about to tread unknown waters. "We haven't had a chance to talk about that yet, have we?"

Cupping her shoulders, he urged her to face him, then grasped her hands. The forlorn look in her eyes tore at his insides. He didn't want to force her to talk about anything that might upset her. But her memory loss was an issue they couldn't evade. It was there, staring them both in the face, every minute of every day. They needed to deal with it. . .so they could move on.

"No," he said, "we haven't. But we need to. Don't you think?"

"Yes." Her shoulder dropped an inch in resignation. "We do." Her gaze skimmed the room, settling on the sofa. "Let's sit down."

He helped her remove and fold the sheet covering the sofa, then tossed it over the arm of a linen-covered chair.

They settled on the couch facing each other: she with her hands clasped in her lap, one leg tucked beneath her; he with one arm folded over the back of the sofa, a leg bent and resting on the cushion between them.

After only a slight hesitation, she began. "After a battery of tests and a failed attempt at hypnosis, the doctors determined my memory loss was permanent."

He took a moment to digest the information. She would never regain her memory. Her past—and her memory of theirs together—was gone. Forever. What did that mean? For her? For him? For them?

"Are they certain?" he asked, grabbing at a straw he saw slipping far beyond his reach.

She nodded. "The tests were actually just protocol. Their final diagnosis was based on the type of head injuries I sustained."

He'd half expected, half anticipated this. But the reality still hit him full force, like an unforeseen sucker punch to the chest.

She ducked her head and studied her hands. "Daniel, I know you had hoped my memory would return. . ." Pausing, she pursed her lips, then lifted a misty gaze back to his. He could see she was fighting tears. "I'm sorry," she added, as though that was the only thing left to say.

Seeing her struggle overrode his own confusion and pain, giving him the strength to offer her the comfort she needed. The comfort he owed her.

He cupped her cheek with his hand. "Lydia, you don't owe anyone an apology for what happened to you. Especially me." Forcing nonchalance into his voice, he added, "So, your memory will never return. We'll deal with it. The important thing is, it doesn't change the way I feel about you." He took a few heartbeats to scan her face, giving himself enough time to steel the courage to seek his next answer. "I guess the next thing we need to figure out is how you feel about me."

She raised a cool palm and covered the hand pressed against her face. "Oh, Daniel, I know I have feelings for you, and that those feelings run deeper than anything my limited memory has ever known." She gave her head a slow, regretful shake. "But right now, I have no idea who Lydia Quinn really is. Who *I* am." A long second drifted by. "I'm going to do my best to figure that out, but it's going to take time. How long? I don't know." Her eyes pleaded with his for understanding. "Are you willing to wait?"

"Of course, I'll wait," he said without hesitation. He'd waited five years to find her. He'd wait five more to win back her love if he had to. "I wasn't planning on going anywhere anyway," he added.

A garbled sound—half laughter, half sob—escaped her throat. Her arms reached out to circle his neck.

With a sigh of acceptance, Daniel enfolded her in his

embrace. She had feelings for him. *Deep* feelings, she had said. He closed his eyes. He wanted more. So much more. But he knew what she was offering today was all she could give. For now, that would have to be enough.

Her sweet scent made him long to claim her lips, taste the sweetness in her kiss. But he quelled the urge to do more than simply hold her. He would wait. Because he knew, when he finally earned her love, that wait, no matter how long, would be well worth it.

twelve

"What do you think about this?" Lydia held up the dark pantsuit for her customer's approval.

With a disapproving frown, Mrs. Pratt shook her head. "I don't know about the navy, dear. Do you have something a little more colorful?"

Lydia managed to hold onto her smile. "I think so." She hung up the pantsuit and for the third time searched the garment rack in an attempt to find the mayor's wife a suitable outfit to wear to an upcoming Fourth of July celebration.

Lydia had been back in Quinn Island for a month, back working in the shop for three weeks. And for two weeks and six days, she had hated her job. Hated it. . .with a passion.

She hated trying to figure out which garments suited the tastes of Quinn Island's finest. And she hated it when, nine times out of ten, her patrons looked down their nose at her selection.

She hated wearing ridiculously expensive, and usually uncomfortable, clothes in order to blend in with the atmosphere of the store. And she hated that the mother in an average-to-low income household couldn't come into the shop and purchase a simple Sunday dress for her daughter without spending an entire week's wages.

But the thing she hated most about being the sole owner of an affluent dress shop was leaving Chloe behind in the mornings.

In Chicago, Lydia had been able to take her daughter with her on her housecleaning jobs. Determined to follow the same pattern here, she had set up a children's entertainment center in one corner of the store equipped with television,

VCR, toys, and books. The play area helped in occupying young children brought into the store by their parents for short periods of time. But, halfway through Lydia's first day on the job, Chloe had gotten bored and restless. She didn't like being restricted to the four waist-high walls designed to look like a playhouse. And Lydia would often dash back to check on her daughter while waiting on a customer—which didn't set too well with her clientele.

She'd finally relented and taken her parents up on their offer to watch over her daughter during shop hours. To Lydia's dismay Chloe was thrilled. Lydia's parents—especially her mother—were constantly showering their granddaughter with gifts, taking her to fun places, doing things with her that had always been beyond Lydia's means.

Lydia paused, considering a flamingo-colored pantsuit. Deciding Mrs. Pratt wouldn't look good in pink, she moved on.

So far, Chloe's daily adventures with her grandparents didn't seem to be spoiling her. But Lydia feared it was just a matter of time. Oh, she had told her parents they were indulging their granddaughter too much, and her father seemed to take her concerns to heart most of the time. But her mother *never* listened to, or else she simply chose to ignore, Lydia's requests. And Lydia hadn't quite figured out what to do about it yet.

Turning, she held up a red outfit for Mrs. Pratt's approval. The woman, whose patience seemed to be wearing thin, shook her haughty head again.

Lydia gritted her teeth, biting back a sharp retort. She thought the pleasingly plump woman with the peaches-and-cream complexion would look good in the red.

Pivoting back to the rack, Lydia continued with her search. Why did the women who visited the shop feel she or Jennifer or one of the clerks had to help them make their selections anyway? Didn't anyone in this town have a mind of her own?

On a whim, she whipped out the flamingo pantsuit she'd passed up a minute ago. Mrs. Pratt had already snubbed three of Lydia's choices. What was one more?

To Lydia's surprise, the woman's eyes lit up like headlights on high beam. "That's it." She grabbed the matching garments from Lydia's hand. "Wait right here and you can tell me how it looks after I try it on." With that, she did an about-face and shuffled to the dressing room.

Lydia gave serious thought to hiding beneath the garments hanging on the rack. She didn't want to give her opinion on the pink pantsuit, because she'd have to lie in order not to offend Quinn Island's first lady.

Like a perceptive angel of mercy, Jennifer appeared at Lydia's side. "You have a phone call, Sis."

Lydia looked heavenward and mouthed, "Thank You, God. Thank You." Then she faced her sister with an elated smile. "You don't mind finishing up with Mrs. Pratt, do you?"

The corners of Jennifer's lips turned down. "I knew I should have taken a message."

Lydia made her escape as Mrs. Pratt came out of the dressing room. "Oh, Jennifer, dear," Lydia heard the mayor's wife say. "If I had known you were here. . ."

With a subtle grin, Lydia circled the counter. Couldn't Jennifer see that *her* name belonged on the deed and ownership papers of the shop? Not Lydia's?

Sitting down on a stool behind the counter, she kicked off her two-inch heels. As she reached for the receiver, she crossed her legs and massaged one foot with her free hand. She had yet to figure out the reason for wearing pinching shoes for the sake of style.

"Hello. This is Sa. . .Lydia Quinn." How many more times was she going to do that? "May I help you?"

"Miss Quinn, this is Andy Kelley at Kelley's Used Cars. I'm just calling to let you know your car's been serviced and is ready for pick up."

Excitement kicked up a little dance beneath Lydia's ribs. Her car. *Her* car. The sweet little white number she'd closed the deal on last Friday was ready to pick up. Come tomorrow, she'd no longer have to depend on everyone else for transportation. She could chart her own course.

"Thank you, Mr. Kelley. I'll be there first thing in the morning to pick it up."

She hung up the phone, only vaguely still aware of her hurting feet. The timing was perfect. Tomorrow was her Wednesday off. And Daniel, who had just finished a time-consuming court case, was taking half the day off to spend with her and Chloe. Since they had made no definite plans, Lydia could pick him up and they could drive to the island for a picnic. Wouldn't he be surprised? She couldn't wait to see the look on his face when he saw what she had done.

The front door chimed, and Lydia glanced toward the entrance to see that another patron had arrived. She jumped off the stool and was halfway around the counter when she realized she could feel the coolness of the hardwood floors beneath her feet. She ran back behind the counter, slipped her shoes on, then headed for the front of the store, greeting her next customer with an enthusiastic smile.

&

"Thanks, Dad. For everything," Lydia told her father the next morning as she stepped up to her new used car. Last week, he had helped her pick out, test-drive, and examine the mid-size station wagon for operating efficiency. Today, he had driven her to the dealer to pick up the car.

She always had such fun with him. He was easygoing, sometimes funny, and would always share his knowledge when asked for advice. But he never insinuated he knew what she should like or what was best for her.

Like Mrs. Porter had always done, he simply let her be.

"Anytime, sweetheart. All you have to do is ask whenever you need me."

She kissed his cheek, then looked down at Chloe, who stood beside her granddad, holding onto his forefinger while nestling George the Giraffe under one arm. "Are you ready to go?"

Chloe cocked her head and peered at her mother through the sunglasses Daniel had given her the first day they had gone to the island. "Are you sure you know how to drive?"

Chloe had never seen her mother drive. In order to obtain a driver's license, one had to have proof of existence—a birth certificate, a social security card. Lydia had none of those things in Chicago.

But she had remedied that just last week. Plopping her fists on her hips, she leaned over so that she was practically nose-to-nose with her daughter. "I passed the driver's exam and got my license back, didn't I?"

Chloe pushed her glasses up on her nose and readjusted George. "Yes," she said, but her expression still looked a little wary around the edges.

After fastening Chloe in the car, Lydia kissed her father's cheek again and climbed in. Heat and humidity were already beginning to weigh down the late June morning. But when Lydia switched on the engine, instead of reaching for the air conditioner button, she pressed the control that zipped down the window. She wanted to feel and smell the fresh air as she drove *her* car for the first time.

At the beginning of her search for an automobile to suit hers and Chloe's needs, Lydia and her father had scavenged the new-car lots. But she had soon concluded it was senseless to pay five figures for a car that would depreciate several thousand dollars the minute she drove it off the lot. So she had settled for a two-year-old, average-sized, averaged-priced, four-door station wagon with a gray cloth interior and bright, white exterior. A car that had Sara Jennings's name written all over it.

No, she retracted her thoughts with a mental shake of her

head. The car had *Lydia Quinn*'s name written all over it.

She shifted into drive. No matter how hard she tried, she still sometimes had trouble thinking of herself as *Lydia,* Quinn Island's former prom queen, instead of *Sara,* Chicago's plain Jane Doe.

When she first pulled out onto the highway, her pulse quickened. But a couple miles into the trip, she was navigating the steering wheel like driving was second nature.

She stopped at the supermarket deli and picked up a lunch of fried chicken, fries, slaw, and banana pudding. On the way to the checkout, she grabbed a six-pack of soft drinks and some eating utensils. The reporters had finally stopped hounding her, and the townspeople had all gotten used to the news of her return, so she got in and out of the store with just a few polite greetings and inquiries as to how she and Chloe were doing. But, even if she had had to sidestep a member of the news media, the feeling of freedom would have been worth it.

At precisely twelve-thirty, Lydia pulled into the driveway of Daniel's one-level brick home. When she saw his car still sitting beneath the carport, she knew she had timed her arrival just right. She'd given him enough time to get home from his office and change clothes, but had caught him before he left to come and pick up her and Chloe.

As she and Chloe climbed out of the car, he ambled out of the front door, letting the screen door slap closed behind him. He approached with slow, curious steps. Lydia stopped beside Chloe's door, took off her sunglasses, and just watched him. The blazing midday sun lit chestnut highlights in his dark hair. His yellow polo shirt molded his sinewy shoulders, and his faded jeans could have been tailor-made to fit his slim waist and thighs.

Instead of stopping where she and Chloe stood, he continued on, strolling around the car with his hands in his pockets. A guarded look of bewilderment settled over his face.

When he had made a complete circle, he stopped in front

of her. "What is this?"

Feeling about as proud of herself as a peacock, Lydia stuffed her fists in her overall pockets and rocked back on her heels. "It's my new car. Ya like it?"

Daniel scratched his forehead with his thumb. "Ah, when did you get it?"

She noticed he had evaded her question, which knocked her elation down a couple of notches. "Bought it last week. Picked it up this morning."

"All by yourself?"

She feigned offense. "What? You don't think I know cars? This baby has a V-6 engine, automatic transmission with automatic overdrive, antilock front and rear disk brakes, and gets twenty-nine miles to the gallon on the highway." She shuffled from one end of the car to the other like a seasoned salesperson while she shot off the list she had practiced with her father. And when she stopped, pivoted, and beamed at Daniel, she was pleased with the results.

His mouth dropped open like a trapdoor with a broken hinge. "Where did you learn all that?"

"From Grandpa."

Lydia's smugness fizzled like a drop of water hitting a hot skillet. She glowered down at her daughter. "Thank you, Chloe. I was really anxious to let Daniel know that."

Unperturbed, the informative four-year-old simply pushed her glasses back up on her nose.

Reluctantly, Lydia lifted her gaze to Daniel's face. Just as she expected, he was smirking.

"Your dad helped you pick out the car."

She lifted her nose an impertinent inch. "We picked it out together."

He scanned the vehicle again, front to back. "Why didn't you tell me you were buying a car?"

"I wanted to surprise you." And, even though she loved him—and she did love him, with every fiber of her being—

she didn't want to be influenced by his sometimes aggressive decisiveness.

He scratched his forehead with his thumb again. "You surprised me all right."

Like a factory inspector, he ambled around to the driver's side, opened the door, checked the mileage and all the control gadgets—half of which Lydia still hadn't figured out. He requested the keys, then switched on the engine, and revved the motor. While the car was running, he checked the heat, the air conditioner, and the radio. Switching off the engine, he pulled a lever that popped open the hood, then got out and scrutinized the conglomeration of metal called a motor. Seemingly satisfied with what he saw, he closed the hood and got down on his hands and knees, looking underneath the car.

All the things her father had done when she'd expressed an interest in the vehicle.

Standing, he brushed off his knees and then his hands. "Nice car. Been well taken care of," he said, but it was what he didn't say that bugged her.

Crossing her arms, she shifted her weight to one leg. "What is it, Daniel?"

"Nothing," he said with all the innocence of a car thief.

She had learned enough about him to know when he was holding back on her. Tilting her head to one side, she leveled him with an unbending glare.

He opened his mouth to speak.

She pursed her lips.

His shoulders dropped in resignation. "I like the car, Lydia, I really do. It's just that—"

She held up a hand. "Wait a minute. Don't tell me it's not me. If I hear one more person say something's not me, I'll scream."

With a spark of amusement in his eyes, he grinned. "We wouldn't want you to do that, now, would we?"

She found herself smiling in return. "No. I don't think we would."

He crouched down to give Chloe his usual hug and nuzzle on the cheek. Sometimes, Lydia envied that little affectionate greeting from Daniel that belonged only to her daughter. All she ever got was his hand on hers or an arm slipped casually around her.

She appreciated Daniel's modest patience in courting her, but, good grief, didn't the twentieth date or so warrant at least a good-night kiss?

"I smelled food in the car," he said as he stood. "Does that mean we're going on a picnic?"

"How does an afternoon on the island sound?"

"Sounds like my kind of date."

While he helped Chloe with her seat, Lydia skirted the front of the car and slid into the driver's seat.

Daniel opened the passenger door and poked his head inside. Arching his brows, he said, "You mean you're not going to let me drive?"

Caressing the steering wheel, she shook her head. "Not just yet. I feel like I've just gotten my first set of wings and I still want to fly."

She noticed a subtle change in his expression; the slightest hint of sadness rose in his eyes. "As long as you always let me fly with you." He folded himself into the passenger seat and closed the door.

Despite the elevated temperature, a chill raced down her spine. Something was wrong. She sensed it.

When he grasped her chin between his thumb and forefinger, leaned over, and pressed the softest of kisses to her forehead, she pushed her misgivings to a remote corner of her mind. *We're okay,* she told herself with forced conviction. *We're still okay.*

On the drive to the island, he started snooping, poking around in her dash pocket, thumbing through the owner's manual, studying the service record left by the last owner. But, Lydia noticed, he was quiet. Too quiet. And somber.

"Daniel, what is it about my getting this car that bothers you so?"

✌

He kept his gaze focused on the owner's manual he held open in his hands. He knew it was petty, a grown man getting his feelings hurt because the woman he loved hadn't told him she was buying a car. But he couldn't seem to help it. She had once made him a part of her every decision. Lately, though, she was making more and more choices without consulting him. Sometimes, like right now, an ornery little monster would rear its ugly little head and set him to wondering if she'd eventually get to where she didn't need him at all.

"Daniel?" she gently prodded when he didn't answer.

He certainly wasn't going to tell her he was sitting there licking his wounds, so to speak. But he could ask her one thing. He returned the owner's manual to the dash pocket and closed it. All he'd really wanted to do anyway was make sure she hadn't forgotten proof of insurance. "I was just wondering why you bought this particular car?"

"It's practical for me and Chloe. It's in good running condition. It was reasonably priced."

It was practical for *her* and *Chloe*. Did he not fit into her picture anywhere? "But you could have bought any car you wanted."

"And I did."

He considered her answer. Before, she would never have settled for a used car, or one that she'd considered so "average." He raked his hair away from his forehead and heaved a sigh. That didn't seem to be the case anymore.

He studied her hauntingly familiar yet somehow-new profile. Since her return, she was always doing things that sometimes surprised him, sometimes shocked him, and many times delighted him. Her former tastes for expensive toys had never really bothered him before, not much, anyway. After all, they both came from old money and had profitable jobs. They could afford it. But her more recent tastes for practical, more functional essentials with reasonable price tags charmed him—and paralleled his own way of thinking.

"What are you going to do with your other car?" he asked, referring to the sports coupe she'd been driving the night of her abduction. Right now, it was in her uncle's basement garage, where it had been towed after the initial police investigation.

"I'm going to sell it and give the proceeds to the missing persons' organization my mother founded." She shrugged a shoulder. "Who knows? Maybe the money will help locate another lost loved one."

His level of respect for her increased twofold. Reaching over, he laced his fingers through hers, leaving her with only one hand to drive. "Since when did you get to be so amazing?"

She didn't have an immediate comeback, and he couldn't help grinning. The way she now blushed at compliments was so appealing.

"Maybe. . .since I met you," she finally said, and started working her fingers free from his. "Now, give me back my hand before I run off the road."

thirteen

"Mr. Matthews, you have magic hands."

Daniel smiled at the woman lying back against the settee arm, her eyes closed, looking thoroughly satisfied with the foot rub she was getting. "And you, Miss Quinn, have beautiful feet." Small and dainty. They fit perfectly in his hands.

"Mmm," was her only response.

Feeling quite relaxed himself, he settled further down on the sofa and propped his bare feet on an ottoman.

The afternoon had been glorious. They had eaten out on the back lawn, then taken a quick swim to combat the scorching temperatures. When Chloe had worn down, they had returned to the cottage, changed from swimsuits back to their street clothes, and tucked the little girl into the same bed she'd slept in the first time Daniel had brought her and Lydia to the island.

Laying his head back, Daniel scanned the living room of the cottage, which was beginning to look and feel more like a home than a house that had been forsaken for seven years. They had removed the linens from the furniture on their second visit and spruced up the yards on their third. Last week, Lydia had added a few personal touches—scented candles to the coffee table, a ginger jar to the mantle, and a silk flower arrangement to the dining room table. Today, she had brought a crocheted afghan and thrown it across the wicker rocking chair that sat next to the fireplace.

Little things that make a house a home, Daniel thought. And with just a little nudge to his imagination, he could picture this house as a home: his, Lydia's, and Chloe's.

With a circling thumb, he started working his way up from

Lydia's heel. She shifted and gave a contented purr. He loved pleasing her, and since she'd returned to Quinn Island, that had been amazingly easy to do. The simplest things—a walk on the beach, a single red rose, an unexpected foot rub— brought her pleasure now.

His smile mellowed. She had been so flabbergasted, and so appealingly embarrassed, the first time he'd pulled her feet into his lap, slipped off her shoes, and started massaging. And so appreciative afterward. He couldn't have been more shocked than when she pulled his feet into her lap and returned the favor.

Mentally, he shook his head. That had been a first. But then, there had been a lot of firsts since her return. Some pleased him. But some he didn't quite know what to do with, like her showing up at his house today with a car she'd picked out and purchased without his knowledge.

He pushed the nagging thought to the back of his mind. Wasn't it enough to simply be with her like this? Something stirred inside him—a deeper longing, a stronger need. He struggled against the desire to move his hands to her slim ankles, to lean over her and satisfy his hunger with one sweet kiss.

She had given him no indication she was ready to move their relationship forward. What they presently had would have to be enough. . .for now.

She flinched when he hit a particularly sensitive spot in the middle of her foot. "Hey, no tickling," she chided, opening her eyes to level him with a halfhearted glare.

Just to see her eyes dance with laughter and feel her small toes curl beneath his fingers, he kept circling the end of his thumb in the center of her foot. Just before she reached the point of squirming, she jerked her feet away.

"You don't play fair."

He helped her sit up. "I couldn't resist," he said.

"No. You just wanted your own feet rubbed." Facing him,

she scooted back, folded one leg in front of her, and patted her thigh.

Who was he to argue? Taking her cue, he propped one foot on her bent knee. She set to kneading, her smooth brow pinched in concentration.

He watched in fascination. He would have never thought that a woman rubbing a man's feet could be so enthralling. Of course, this wasn't just any woman. This was Lydia, and she was what made this simple act of altruism so attractive. He relaxed back against the sofa arm.

"Daniel," Lydia said as she started working on his other foot, "if this house were yours, would you move into it?"

"In a heartbeat," he answered without hesitation.

Her frown of concentration melted into a warm smile. "Good."

His brow dipped in befuddlement. "Why?"

She glanced up at him, her amber eyes all aglow. "Because I've decided to move out here."

Her answer brought him up short. He pulled his feet away from her hands and slid forward, his knee bumping lightly against hers as he draped his arm over the back of the couch. "Are you serious?"

Annoyance wilted her shoulders. "Daniel."

"I know. I know. If you hear 'Are you serious?' one more time, you're going to scream. But. . .are you serious?" His voice squeaked with surprise.

She shook her head like he was a hopeless cause. "Yes, I am. Why does that surprise you so?"

"I don't know." But really he did. She had been totally against living on the island in the past. She hated the feel of salt on her skin, the wind in her hair, and the quiet seclusion. "I guess because you liked living in town so much before. You were a people person."

She took a moment to consider his answer. "Well, I've changed my mind." From the tilt of her lips, she apparently found his stunned expression amusing. "That is a woman's prerogative, isn't it?"

"I suppose, but. . ."

"But?"

"You'll be so far away from everything."

"Just three miles from town."

"And it's so secluded out here. Suppose there's a break-in?"

"You said the island was the safest place on the coast."

"Well, yeah, but. . .what if Chloe gets sick?"

"I have a car. I know how to use the phone."

He opened his mouth, but, for the life of him, couldn't think of another justifiable argument.

She grinned in victory.

He scowled in defeat.

He knew he had a tendency to be overprotective, as she had so gently pointed out on several different occasions. But he couldn't help it. The thought of her being out here alone gripped his stomach with fear. What if something happened to her or Chloe? He couldn't go through losing Lydia again. And with Chloe in the picture, the stakes were now twice as high.

She bracketed his head with her hands and leaned forward until her face was only a breath away from his. "Daniel, I'm not a child. I'm a grown woman, with a child of my own."

He couldn't argue with that. Still, he had his reservations. "I know. It's just the thoughts of you and Chloe being out here all by yourself. . ." An old familiar weight bore down on his chest. "Sometimes, things can happen. . *fast*. When you least expect them to. I'm entitled to be concerned."

Understanding softened her features. "I know. But you can't live in fear that something bad is going to happen every time I get out of your sight. And you can't put me and Chloe in a bubble and shield us from the world. Now, I can promise you I will do everything possible to ensure my and Chloe's safety." A knowing glint of laughter flickered across her lips. "And,

I'm sure you will, too." Then the laughter was gone. She spread her fingers, as though trying to encompass his mind and conquer his fears. "The rest we have to leave up to God."

He closed his eyes, his insides quaking with the struggle between past demons and present rationality. Somehow, rationality won. "You're right," he begrudgingly admitted as he opened his eyes. "I can't lock you and Chloe away, and I can't be with you every minute of every day. But. . ." He scrubbed a defeated hand down his face, then desperately grabbed at one last straw. "How would you feel about me parking a camper in your backyard?"

She threw her head back and laughed. The infectious sound managed to calm, to a small degree, his inner turmoil.

He offered her a sheepish grin. He knew parking a camper in her backyard wasn't reasonable. But he'd do it, if she'd let him.

Following instinct, he pulled her close and wrapped his arms around her. She slipped hers around his neck. He could live to be a hundred and never get tired of the feel of her body in his arms.

She raised a hand, combed her fingers through the back of his hair. Jolted by a strong need for more, he closed his eyes. Why didn't he just go ahead and kiss her? The worst thing that could happen would be for her to push him away, like she did that first day in Chicago.

He drew back, cupped the side of her face with his hand, and before he even had a chance to act upon his thoughts, she pushed him away.

"Oh, Daniel. Look!" She jumped up and breezed past him.

It took him a few seconds to adjust to the change in atmosphere. When he did, he twisted around to find she had opened the back door and was kneeling down to pick up something, her abundant curls fluttering in the breeze. She stood, and when she turned around, she was holding a kitten—if you could call it that. The neglected little thing looked more like two huge yellow eyes sewn into a scraggly coat of matted gray fur.

As though pleading for mercy, the haggard feline looked at him and released a weak "Meow."

"Poor baby." Lydia cradled the kitten against her chest as gently as a mother would a newborn. "She's scared to death and starving."

Standing, Daniel rubbed the back of his forefinger beneath the kitten's chin. The kitten turned her head and flattened her ear against his hand, touching a soft spot inside him. "I think Chloe had some milk left over from lunch. I'll go see if I can dig up a pan and warm it up."

While they waited in the kitchen for the milk to heat, Daniel watched Lydia lavish the kitten with attention. She set the scrawny thing down on the bar, then plopped her chin on folded hands so that she and the animal were eye level. The cat arched her bony body along Lydia's face, then it sniffed at Lydia's hair and was knocked backwards by a sneeze. Laughing out loud, Lydia picked up the stunned kitten and rubbed her cheek against the top of its fuzzy head.

Daniel stood awestruck. Lydia had apparently forgotten she hated cats. She didn't like animals, period. She detested getting fur on her clothes. Bemusement tugging at the corner of his mouth, he turned back to the stove and poured the milk into a bowl. He certainly wasn't going to be the one to remind her of that fact.

Five minutes later, they sat side by side on the floor, their legs crisscrossed, watching the kitten devour the warm milk.

"Where do you think she came from?" Lydia wondered out loud.

"My guess is some heartless jerk set her out thinking somebody here on the island would take her in. . .or that she'd starve to death."

The light in Lydia's eyes grew dim. "Poor thing." Reaching out with a forefinger, she ruffled the fur on the kitten's back.

"Lost, alone, no place to call home." A brief silence filled with heavy thoughts passed. "I know exactly how you feel."

Daniel curled a finger beneath Lydia's chin and urged her to look at him. "You're not lost anymore."

Bitter tears stung her eyes. "Sometimes, I wonder. . ." The second the words were out, she drew back and swiped a hand across her face. She hadn't gotten through the last five years by crying on someone else's shoulder or playing off another's sympathy. And she certainly wasn't going to start now. "Sorry. I didn't mean to whine."

Apparently undeterred, Daniel grasped her chin and forced her to look at him again. "Lydia, why don't you let me in? Let me help you carry some of that burden while you're trying to figure everything out."

"I'm not a baby, Daniel." Pushing his hand away, she vaulted up off the floor and strolled to the window over the sink. Crossing her arms, she looked out at the waters battering the island's southern shore.

She was angry with herself. In a weak moment of self-pity, she had opened a door she had meant to keep closed. The past, the only one she could remember, was gone. She was no longer Sara Jennings. She was Lydia Quinn. She was *born* Lydia Quinn and, somehow, she had to accept that. She just never realized it would be so hard.

Daniel's hands, so understanding and tender, cupped her shoulders. Following his gentle bidding, she relaxed back against him. His strong arms enfolded her shoulders. She raised her hands to his forearms, laid her head back against his chest. Balmy scents of warm milk, saltwater, and the most intoxicating one of all that belonged only to him drifted through her head, filling her with a selfish yearning. Sometimes, she wished she could shut out the world and create one of her own that included only her, Daniel, and Chloe.

But even as the thought flitted through her mind, her pragmatic side reminded her that kind of thinking was unreasonable. She had responsibilities, people who depended on her, more demands than she could ever possibly meet. And she owed it to her loved ones to try to meet those demands.

Daniel's warm lips touched her temple. "I love you, Lydia. That's one thing you'll never have to try to figure out."

She turned in his arms, letting her palms rest against his chest. "How, Daniel? How can you love some crazy, confused woman who's nothing like the one you fell in love with years ago?"

He touched her nose. "First of all, you're not crazy. Secondly, who can explain love?" He shrugged. "I certainly can't. All I know is that it's still there, stronger than ever. I don't question it; I just accept it."

If he didn't question it, then why should she? Focusing on her hands, she fiddled with a button on his shirt. "Then why don't you ever kiss me?"

He tipped her chin. "Because you asked me to wait."

Her brow dipped in befuddlement. "I did?"

"Uh-huh." He nodded. "Remember the first day we came to the cottage? You asked me to wait until you figured everything out."

Closing her eyes, she pinched the bridge of her nose. "Daniel, I was talking about renewing our engagement. I figured, in the meantime, we would date and. . .you know. . .let our relationship follow the natural course of things."

He grasped the fingers she held to her face and kissed the back of her hand. "Why didn't you say something? Or at least give me a sign?"

She tried to focus more on what he was saying than the chill bumps racing up her arm. "Because I'm a woman," she answered, thinking surely that would explain it all.

Apparently, it didn't. "Yes," he said, his dark eyes roaming her face with a mixture of amusement and appreciation. "I'm well aware of that." He started rocking, carrying her with him in that gentle sway of his that kept time with a song only he and she could hear.

"The man is supposed to make the first move, not the woman."

The rocking stopped, and surprise lifted his brows. "You never felt that way before."

Her eyes opened wide. "What!?"

"Nothing," he quickly injected, then closed his eyes, giving his head a quick shake like he was trying to clear it of a distraction. When he met her gaze again, he added, "Forget I said that." He let go of her hand and captured her wrists, urging her to put her arms around his neck. She didn't resist.

"Now, about this kissing thing." He slipped his arms around her waist. "Seems like I was waiting on you. You were waiting on me."

Biting her lower lip, she nodded. She didn't have enough air to speak.

He pulled her closer. "What are we going to do about it?"

"I guess. . .this."

Following her heart, she rose on tiptoe and lifted her face up to his.

"Mama!"

Chloe's voice coming from the hallway shattered Lydia's moment of rapture. She squeezed her eyes shut against the impact as her emotions slammed back to earth. Then, lowering her heels to the floor, she opened her eyes and pressed a forefinger to Daniel's lips. "Hold that thought. Okay?"

He kissed her fingertip. "Got it."

They parted just before Chloe turned the corner coming into the kitchen, her small hands circling the ribs of the kitten Lydia had long forgotten. The neglected cat looked like she was frozen in a permanent state of shock, but she didn't seem to be in any pain.

Lydia rushed across the room to show her daughter how to hold the kitten properly. Chloe held up the furry, yellow-eyed skeleton and said, "Look what I found, Mama. A kitty cat."

❧

Daniel was still holding onto Lydia's thought when she later drove him home so he could pick up his car and follow her back to her parents' house.

While swapping secretive little glances with Lydia, he suffered through a preplanned dinner at the Quinn's dining room table. Then he sat through an hour of some insipid game show Margaret insisted they watch, her idea of a family thing. Then came Chloe's story time and bedtime which he breezed through with utmost patience.

But after he and Lydia had tucked her daughter in, with kitten Mittens—named for her white front paws—in a basket beside the bed, and closed the bedroom door, he grabbed Lydia's hand, and together they rushed down the stairs like two kids on Christmas morning. They hit the foyer running, but Daniel stopped short when Margaret stepped from the living room into their path. Lydia, who was one step behind him, apparently didn't see the older woman and smacked into his back, almost catapulting him forward to the floor at her mother's feet.

He reached back with his free hand to steady her. "Mrs. Quinn!" *Uh-oh.* He'd called her "Mrs. Quinn" instead of "Margaret." He hadn't done that in years. He sounded just like a kid caught sneaking a cookie before lunch.

Out of the corner of his eye, he saw Lydia peek out from behind his shoulder. "Hi, Mom." Unfortunately, she sounded just as guilty as he.

With a quizzical frown puckering her forehead, Margaret Quinn looked from Daniel to Lydia, then back to Daniel. "Where on earth are you kids going in such a hurry?"

Daniel opened his mouth, but all that came out was a caught-in-the-act-sounding "Ahh." And Lydia was no help. She just stayed under cover behind him.

Then, like a perceptive guardian angel, Lydia's father

appeared. "Come on, Margaret," he said, grasping her hand. "There's something on TV I want you to see." Sending Daniel a conspiratorial wink, the older man pulled his thoroughly perplexed wife back into the living room.

The instant they were out of sight, Daniel and Lydia scrambled for the door.

They sprinted toward the side of the wraparound porch, startling the night creatures into silence. When they rounded the corner, where they knew they would be safe from windows and prying eyes, Daniel leaned back against the wall.

Slightly out-of-breath, he slid his back down the smooth plank wall far enough to compensate for their height differences. "Now, there's this matter of a—"

She grabbed his head and kissed him.

Daniel couldn't move. Couldn't breathe. Couldn't think. All he could do was stand there and receive what she was offering. Her love, without reservation. No, she hadn't actually said the words. But it was there. He could feel her pouring it into him, washing him clean, purest of mountain streams running down from the highest of mountains.

Fireworks exploded in his chest. The doors to his heart, soul, and mind—places that had been only half open before—swung wide open, the emotions flowing out of them. His throat ached.

And when she finally pulled back, looking up at him like he was her lifeline, he saw her in a completely new light. He couldn't explain it; he didn't even know if he wanted to. He just knew that things were different. A lot different than they were before. What he felt for her was deeper and more far-reaching than anything he had ever known.

And as new as the first rose in spring.

"Well," she said, her voice filtering into his awestruck thoughts, "aren't you going to say anything?"

"I'm. . .speechless."

She brushed her thumb across his lower lip. He felt the

tingle all the way to his fingertips.

"There's something I need to tell you," she said. Dropping her hands to his chest, she raised her lashes and looked so deep into his eyes, he could feel her gaze touching his soul. "I may not have myself figured out yet, but I do know how I feel about you."

"I'm listening."

"I love you, Daniel. I love you with all my heart."

He cradled her face in his hands. He couldn't hold back the tears; he didn't even want to try. "Lydia. My precious, precious Lydia, you don't know how I've longed to hear you say that."

Her lips curved. "Well, get used to it, because I have a feeling you're going to be hearing it a lot in the future."

"Good, because I love you." He lowered his head to hers. "I love you," he repeated in a whisper against her mouth before he claimed her lips.

This time, it was he who gave. He willingly laid every fiber of his being in the palm of her hand, holding back nothing for himself.

And when she reached out with her heart to accept his gift, he knew, for the first time in his life, what it felt like to give freely and love without condition.

🦋

Much later that evening, Lydia walked hand in hand with Daniel to his car. "I can't wait until Chloe and I get moved into the cottage," she mused out loud.

"Me, either. That way, we won't risk running into your parents when we're headed out to the front porch to neck."

"*Daniel!*" She smacked his shoulder with her free hand. "We did not neck."

Well, no, really, they hadn't. They'd just kissed, held hands, and each other. But he sure did love making her blush, even if he couldn't quite see the rosy color rising in her cheeks with nothing but stars and a half-moon for light.

He knew it was there.

"Besides," she added, "we'll have an inquisitive four-year-old dogging our every step out at the cottage."

"She goes to bed early."

Lydia shook her head. "You're crazy."

"About you."

Her soft chuckle floated through the air. "I give up."

Her mention of moving to the island reminded him of something he had been curious about since early evening. Stopping next to his car, he urged her to face him and grasped both of her hands. "Tell me something, Lydia. When we were out at the island this afternoon, why did you ask me if I'd move into the cottage if it were mine?"

"Because, if you and I do make it to the wedding altar, I didn't want Chloe and me to move out there, fall more in love with the place than we already are, then have to pull up stakes and move again. Before I made my decision, I needed to know it was a place where you would want to live, too."

"You mean, you didn't make your final decision until you had my answer?"

"No."

Was it possible to love her more? He tugged her into his arms. "Thanks for thinking about me."

"That seems to be about all I do lately."

"Good."

He lingered over a kiss, then held her for a tranquil moment with her head resting against his chest, his cheek resting on the top of her head.

"We're going to make it, Daniel," she said with a sigh. "I have a feeling."

Daniel released a slow breath full of contentment. He had a feeling, too. And it was awesome.

fourteen

"Thanks for allowing me to come in during my lunch break, Daniel. It's Lydia's Wednesday off, and that leaves us a little shorthanded."

"No problem," Daniel said, reaching for the sales contract on a piece of investment property Jennifer had recently acquired. "I should get this wrapped up with the sellers this afternoon. I'll give you a call as soon as everything's finalized."

Nodding, Jennifer stood.

Daniel slipped the contract into her file and reached for the phone, intending to call Lydia to see if she could meet him for lunch. She'd told him she was going to hang new curtains in the cottage today, but surely she could take a break.

But Jennifer lingered, so he stopped short of picking up the receiver and peered up at her. From the worry lines marring her pretty forehead, he could tell something weighed heavily on her mind.

He pulled his hand away from the phone, leaned back in his swivel chair, and laced his hands over his abdomen. "Wanna talk about it?"

"If you've got time."

He really didn't. Allowing her to come in and sign her contract on the spur-of-the-moment hadn't left him much time for lunch, and he really did want to see Lydia. But Jennifer had been there for him so many times over the past five years, he felt he owed her a sympathetic ear whenever she needed one.

He motioned to the chair she had just vacated, and she sat back down. Leaning on her forearms, she focused on her fidgeting red-tipped fingers while she apparently weighed out

143

whatever it was she needed to say.

As patiently as possible, Daniel waited.

Finally, she looked up at him. "Daniel, I was just wondering what you think of Lydia?"

He approached her question with a lawyer's analytical caution. "I'm not sure I understand what you're asking."

"What I'm asking is, what do you think about the way she is now?"

"I still love her, Jen. That's not changed." And that, he thought, explained it all.

"I know, but. . ." She chewed her thumbnail for a long, thoughtful moment before adding, "Does Lydia sometimes do or say things that totally confuse you or catch you off guard?"

His lips curved in a slow grin. "All the time. I mean, sometimes when I'm with her I think I'm looking at Lydia, then she'll do or say something totally out of character, and I feel like I'm seeing someone else." He shook his head, slipping into a daydream filled with visions from the evening before. "When I hold her now, it even feels different."

ðø

Lydia pulled into the parking lot of Matthews and Matthews, Attorneys-at-Law. Since Daniel was working on a property dispute set to go to trial tomorrow, she knew he might not take time for lunch. So, in an impetuous moment, she had decided to lay aside the curtains she was hanging, pick up some takeout, drop by his office, and have lunch with him. Granted, the local burger express didn't specialize in the healthiest food in the world, but at least she would know he'd eaten something to tide him over until their dinner date tonight.

As she parked her station wagon, she noticed Jennifer's car sitting a few spaces away. Her sister was probably there going over paperwork on some new investment. The shrewd businesswoman was always looking for a profitable deal.

Oh, well, Lydia thought as she grabbed the bags from the passenger seat, if Jennifer hadn't eaten, they could all have lunch together. Even though she and Jennifer were as different as night and day, Lydia thoroughly enjoyed her sister's company.

Lydia stepped out of her car, inhaling the boggy, grassy scent of the saltwater marsh across the street. Would she ever come back down to feeling normal again? Not if the last two weeks were any indication of what the future had in store for her. Life had never been so near perfect. She and Chloe had gotten settled into their new home on the island, she was head over heels in love with the most wonderful man in the world, and, for the first time she could remember, she was looking forward to the rest of her life with childlike excitement.

Yes, she thought as she closed the car door, *things are about as perfect as perfect could be.*

As she reached for the entrance door with one hand, she reached for a small part of her that was missing with the other. She felt a little lost not having her daughter along, but the child's grandparents had confiscated her for an afternoon at the park. Since Lydia had planned a day of much work and little play, she had conceded to the outing.

The desk with a missing secretary gave the reception area a lulling out-to-lunch feel. Scanning the doors flanking each side of the workstation, Lydia noted the senior Matthews's door was closed. But Daniel's was standing wide open, which, she knew, meant "Come on in."

Catching her breath in anticipation, she tiptoed across the room.

"Does Lydia sometimes do or say things that totally confuse you or catch you off guard?"

Jennifer's voice, and the mention of her own name, stopped Lydia before she stepped into view of the doorway.

"All the time," came Daniel's answer. "I mean, sometimes

when I'm with her I think I'm looking at Lydia, then she'll do or say something totally out of character, and I feel like I'm seeing someone else." A brief pause, then, "When I hold her now, it even feels different."

Nothing could have prepared Lydia for the forceful blow that knocked her cloud of joy out from under her or for the feeling of her newfound elation hitting the floor with such rock-solid impact. Before her weakening limbs could collapse beneath her, she turned. As quickly and quietly as possible, she left the office.

ஃ

"But, you do think she's all right, don't you?" Jennifer said, continuing her conversation with Daniel. "I mean, you don't think there are any mental repercussions from the attack, do you?"

Daniel noticed that the lines of worry in Jennifer's forehead had deepened. She *really* needed assurance that her sister was going to be all right.

"No, Jen," he said. "With Lydia's permission, I spoke with her doctor and reviewed her medical file. There is no permanent damage other than the memory loss."

Jen's troubled eyes filled with tears. "But she's so different now."

Daniel retrieved a box of tissues from his credenza and offered it to Jennifer, then he leaned forward and folded his arms on his desk. "Jennifer, I don't think anyone can go through what Lydia went though and not be changed. I mean, think about it. She not only lost her memory that night, she lost me, you, your mother and father. Everything that made her what she was, including herself. When she woke up sixteen days later, her entire past, up until that moment, was gone.

"Then, out of sheer survival instinct, I think, she was forced to live as a woman named Sara Jennings for five years. Now, here she is, back on Quinn Island, trying to re-adjust to the life that really belongs to her. She's been jerked around a bit, to say the least, but she's trying hard to adapt, and every day she makes progress." He reached over and patted Jennifer's hand. "She's going to be fine, Jen. She just needs a little more time to figure everything out. That's all."

Jennifer sniffed, dabbing at her eyes with a tissue. "Do you think she'll ever go back to the way she used to be?"

As always, whenever he stopped to ask himself exactly the same question, a niggling fear wormed through him. "I honestly don't know." And he honestly didn't know if he wanted her to.

Pursing her lips, she lowered her gaze. "Can I make a small confession?"

"Attorney-client privilege. Your secret's safe with me."

"There are some things. . .many, really. . .about this new Lydia that I like better."

Me, too, Daniel said to himself. But out of loyalty to the Lydia of his past, he kept the admission to himself. "Lydia will be fine, Jen," he repeated. "You'll see. Just fine."

When Jennifer turned to leave, Daniel checked his watch, then combed a harried hand through his hair. No point in calling Lydia now. His lunch hour was almost over.

&

After dropping her keys twice, she finally managed to unlock the door. Tears streaming, she flew through the house, out the back, stumbled down the steps, and fell to her knees on the beach.

When I hold her now, it even feels different.

The cold, cruel reality in those words almost choked her. She curled her fingers into the gritty sand. Daniel wasn't in love with her. He was in love with a memory.

She looked up to the heavens through bitter tears. The salty breeze stung her wet cheeks. An errant strand of wind-tossed hair plastered her cheek, clung to her mouth. This hurt. Hurt. . .worse than anything.

A sob tore through her body. "Oh, God, help me! *Please,* help me! I don't know who I am anymore."

Burying her face in her gritty hands, she bowed her head to the sand and continued to weep. . .and to pray.

▲

By the time she returned to the house an hour later, she'd cried so many tears, her entire body felt dehydrated. And the back of her neck, she could tell, was sunburned. She pushed her mangled curls away from her face. Maybe she should have just stayed down there and withered away in the sun. It wouldn't have been nearly as painful as facing the brutal reality in Daniel's words less than two hours ago.

She opened the door to a ringing phone. She had a feeling she knew who it was, and she wasn't ready to talk to him yet.

The phone stopped ringing; her recorded greeting played; the tone sounded. "Hi, hon. I just had a minute and thought I'd call. It's been a few hours since I talked to you."

She could hear the grin in his voice. She closed her eyes against the ache in her throat. He had called that morning before he left for work, and everything had been so wonderful then. If she could just roll back the hands of time for a few short hours.

No! She opened her eyes and brought herself up straight. Going back wouldn't do any good. She'd merely be looking at the world through the rose-colored glasses of blind love, and Daniel's heart would still belong to another.

"I guess you decided to go shopping for the cottage after all. If I don't hear from you in an hour or so, I'll ring you back. And, no, I'm not being overprotective and checking up on you. I simply called because I love you."

Anger shot through her like a hurling arrow, and she shivered. "Liar!" she sneered as the phone line went dead, then immediately wanted to recant the sharp retort. Why should she be mad at Daniel? He couldn't help how he felt. He didn't even realize yet he wasn't in love with her.

Like a back draft, another realization hit her. "Oh, God," she whispered through her fingers, "this is going to hurt him.

Just as much as it's hurting me." Her pain heightened. Legs giving way, she crumbled to her knees. The flood of tears started all over again. "Oh, God, what am I going to do?" Wrapping her arms around herself, she began rocking back and forth. "*Please* show me what to do."

Miraculously, she found a small calm in the midst of her storm. And in that silence, a still, small voice spoke to her and told her what to do. Wearily, she picked herself up off the floor, scooping up Mittens as she did so.

A zombielike walk down the hall took Lydia to her bedroom, where an unhung curtain still lay draped over the ironing board. Setting Mittens on the sea-foam-green-and-rose spread that covered her iron bed, she opened her nightstand drawer and withdrew a clothbound book. Testing the feel of its satiny ivory-colored cover, she sat down on the bed. Mittens poked her curious nose over Lydia's arm to see what was so interesting.

Lydia had found the journal among her old belongings when she had taken them out of storage. At the time, she had been surrounded by her family and Daniel, so she'd tucked the book away to read at a more opportune time. She settled back into the mountain of pillows propped against the head rail. Guess this was that time.

Two-and-one-half hours, 177 handwritten pages, and one cup of chamomile tea later, she knew exactly who Lydia was—someone that she herself would never be.

She closed the journal and stared unseeingly at the waves crashing against the jetty beyond her window. "Sara," she whispered.

From beneath the pain of a broken heart, a tiny spark of peace winked at her. Then the window of her soul opened up and revealed the truth to her. *Sara.* That was it. That's who she was.

Not the owner of an elegant dress shop. Not a sophisticated southern belle. Not Quinn Island's golden girl. She was not the woman Daniel Matthews fell in love with all those years ago.

She was Sara. Just plain Sara. And for her, that was enough.

She drew in a shuddery breath. She'd finally figured it out. The sigh that followed was painful. Now, all she had to do was tell Daniel.

Then, she would crawl to some private corner of the world, curl up, and die for a while.

≈

Daniel stood at Lydia's front door, waiting for her to answer the doorbell. He hadn't even gone home to change after work. When she had called thirty minutes ago and said she needed to postpone their dinner date because she wasn't feeling well, he had made a quick trip to the grocery store. He'd picked up soup, saltines, and soft drinks—all those things his mother used to push down his throat whenever he was sick—then driven straight to the cottage.

He shifted the grocery bag from one arm to the other. A full minute had passed. He pushed the doorbell again, shrugging off the uneasiness crawling up his back. Maybe she was in the shower, or maybe she was too sick to get out of bed and answer the door.

He was reaching in his pocket for his key when he heard the shuffle of her small feet.

"Daniel, you shouldn't have come," came her weary-sounding voice through the closed door. "I told you I wasn't feeling well."

"I just wanted to check on you, see if you needed anything."

"No. I don't! I just need to be left alone."

He flinched at her sharp tone. Something was wrong. *Very* wrong. And he wasn't going anywhere until he found out what.

"Daniel," she pleaded, her voice now sounding weak and defeated. "Please. . .just go home."

Didn't she know him better than that? "Lydia, I'm not leaving until you open the door and let me see for myself how you are."

Silence stretched tauter than a harp string.

"I have a key," he reminded her, and he was about to use it when he heard the latch give from the other side. Slowly, she opened the door, and what he saw almost bowled him over. Her hair was a mess, and she was dressed in a long, white, terry robe and fuzzy pink slippers. And she had been cry-ing—hard. "Lydia. What's wrong?"

She stood, one hand still on the doorknob, the other fisted tightly at her side. Was that fury smoldering in her eyes? "I. . . told. . .you. . .I'm. . .not. . .feeling. . .well," she ground out through clenched teeth.

"I'd say that's an understatement." He pushed his way inside, almost tripping over Mittens. Closing the door, he set his loaded grocery bag on the floor and captured Lydia's forearms. His gut twisted at the sight of her tear-swollen eyes. "Talk to me."

She pulled away, as though his touch had burned her. Cupping her elbows, she took several backward steps. As she did so, Daniel sensed her erecting some sort of wall between them. But why?

Something dark and foreboding swept over him, leaving him chilled to the core. Cautiously, he took a step forward.

She took another back. Sorrowfully shaking her head, she said, "I don't want to do this tonight, Daniel. I'm not prepared."

He lifted his hands in a helpless gesture. "Do what, Lydia? For heaven's sake, tell me what's going on!"

A tremor shuddered through her body. Biting down hard on her lower lip, she closed her eyes.

He longed to reach for her, comfort her. But he sensed, somehow, if he did, she'd just slip farther away, farther behind whatever impenetrable wall she was building between them.

When her trembling ceased, she opened her eyes, turned, and wandered to a double window overlooking the sea. Slowly, he followed, stopping an arm's span behind her.

Seconds passed like hours. Daniel fought the choking hand of dread reaching for his throat. His hands sweat; his lungs burned; his head hurt. He didn't know what was coming, only that it was bad.

Finally, she said, "I've finally figured out who Lydia is."

In light of the uneasy currents ricocheting around them, he knew better than to say *That's good*. He somehow swallowed around the sticky dryness in his throat. "And?"

"It's not me."

He willed her to look at him, but he got no results. "What do you mean, it's not you?"

"Just exactly what I said. I'm not now, nor will I ever be, Lydia."

He trapped his temples between his thumb and second finger, trying to keep his reeling mind from crashing. "This doesn't make sense."

"It makes perfect sense if you stop to think about it. I don't act like Lydia; I don't think like Lydia; I don't like the same things Lydia liked." Her face was void of emotion and her body as rigid as a mannequin. It was clear she was trying not to feel. *Forcing* herself not to feel.

"I don't want to be a shop owner," she droned on like a robot. "I want to be an advocate for missing and abused children. I don't want someone telling me how I should dress or wear my hair; I want to decide those things for myself. I don't want to have to recoil every time I have something to say; I want to speak my mind without worrying that I'm going to offend someone every time I do so. I don't want to live in a town house; I want to live right here on the island for the rest of my life."

She finally stopped to take a breath.

"Do you think any of that matters to me?" he ground out.

"It should. It should matter a great deal to you." Her stoic features softened and her rigid shoulders dropped slightly. But she still refused to look at him. "Daniel," she said in a voice now laced with compassion, "five years ago, on that deserted Darlington highway, Lydia died. Sixteen days later,

Sara was born. You didn't ask for it, and neither did I, but that's the way it is." Finally, she turned her head and looked at him, and the depth of pain in her eyes almost ripped him in two. "Lydia's gone, Daniel. I can't replace her. I've accepted that. Now you have to."

He shook his head in denial. "No way. This isn't right."

"Don't you see, Daniel? It's the only thing that is right. Everything else has been wrong up until now."

Fear as quick and sharp as a two-edged sword sliced through him. He pulled a face in disbelief. "What are you saying, Lydia? That you really don't love me?"

No, she wasn't saying that. She would never be able to say that. But she couldn't let him know it.

She turned back to the window. She was dying inside, and she needed to get him away from her. "I'm saying you need to go home and mourn Lydia, Daniel. Go home, and mourn the woman you really love."

He raised his hand.

She closed her eyes. "Please don't touch me," she said quickly, before he had a chance to. Because if he did, she'd shatter into a million pieces around his feet. Then she'd allow him to pick her up and put her back together again, regardless of the cost to her and to him.

When she mentally felt him withdraw his hand, she opened her eyes and continued staring out the window. But out of the corner of her eye, she could see his chest rising and falling with emotion. It took every ounce of willpower she possessed to hold back the tears filling her eyes.

"Okay," he said, then paused to take two more heavy breaths, like he needed them to replenish his strength. "You want me to go; I'll go. For now. But as soon as I figure out what happened between now and this morning, I'll be back. You can count on that, Lydia."

"Sara. My name is Sara."

He just stood there, chest heaving, hands clenching and

unclenching, staring at her like he didn't know what to do with himself.

She had to get him out. Now, before she broke. "You may hate me for this now, Daniel," she said softly. "But someday you'll thank me. Now, *please.* Go."

He captured her chin and forced her to look at him. What she saw in his eyes was both frightening and promising. Anger, confusion, and pain were mixed together with love and determination.

"Hate you?" he said, his voice full of harsh incredulity. "Sweetheart, I will *never* hate you. You can call yourself Sara, Jane, Polly, Sue. Pick one; I don't care." His grip on her chin tightened, stopping short of the point of pain. "I'm not in love with your name; I'm in love with you."

She almost reached out and grabbed the fragile thread of hope he was dangling in front of her. Almost. But just in time he dropped his hand, leaving her weak and incredibly weary.

"Now, I'm going to leave," he added, his hand now clenched back at his side. "Because I'm afraid if I don't, I'm either going to throttle you or knock a hole in your wall. But I'll be back. *Soon.* And that, my dear Sara Jane Polly Sue, is a promise." With that, he turned and stalked away.

She stood by the window and waited until she heard him drive away, then waited a few minutes more. When she was certain he wasn't coming back, certain he wouldn't come in and see her, she buried her face in her hands and crumpled to the floor.

෭

One-and-one-half hours later, Daniel walked out of the Quinns' home, climbed into his car, and headed home. Maybe he should feel guilty that he had just conspired with Lydia's entire family to find out what was going on with her, but he didn't.

He was a desperate man.

fifteen

"Hi, Bill. Come on in." Daniel stepped back to allow the older man entry. "Have you talked to Lydia today?"

Bill shook his head. "Not today. I drove out to see her last night, but she's still not talking."

Daniel's stomach churned with disappointment. It had been three days since his and Lydia's perplexing parting. So far, no one had been able to get her to open up about what had happened that day to make her suddenly turn around and head in the other direction. She would open her door to her family, but not her heart. To Daniel, she would open neither, and it was driving him crazy. He was on the verge of claiming insanity and camping out on her doorstep.

"I did receive a call from Chicago this morning, though," Bill added.

Daniel arched his brows. "Mrs. Porter?" Lydia's friend had gone home several weeks ago; why hadn't he thought of her? If anyone could get through to Lydia, it was her former landlady. "Has Lydia talked to her?"

Bill nodded. "Mrs. Porter called her yesterday, just to see how she was doing."

"And?"

Bill grinned. "Why don't you ask me to sit down? Then I'll tell you what she said."

Chagrined at his lapse in manners, Daniel muttered, "Sorry," and led the way to the den. He'd been doing a lot of peculiar things over the past three days.

Bill settled on a forest-green leather sofa, and Daniel perched on the edge of a matching recliner seat, elbows on knees, hands clasped in front of him.

"Seems like. . .*Sara* overheard a conversation between you and Jennifer on Wednesday that made her feel you were disappointed in the woman she'd become since her abduction."

Daniel's brow creased in concentration. He had to jiggle his memory in order to recall his Wednesday meeting with Jennifer. "Jennifer came into the office that day to sign some papers. We did talk a bit about Lydia, but Lydia wasn't there."

"Yes, she was. Standing right outside your door."

"Eavesdropping?" Daniel couldn't believe it.

"No. At least not intentionally. She'd come to bring you lunch, but when she heard her sister ask you if she ever did things to confuse you, and you told Jen 'yes,' that even holding her was different now, she left."

"I also told Jen that my love for Lydia hasn't changed. Didn't she hear that, too?"

"Guess not."

Daniel flopped back in his chair. "So that's what this is all about. A simple misunderstanding."

Bill shook his head. "I'm not sure it's all that simple."

"Sure, it is. As soon as I explain to her that she didn't hear the whole conversation, she'll realize she jumped to the wrong conclusion, and we'll probably have a good laugh over it." After he kissed her until their breath was gone. But he didn't think her father would be interested in hearing about that.

Bill leveled Daniel with a somber look. "Did she jump to the wrong conclusion, Daniel?"

"Of, course, she did. What else could it be?"

"Perception. Insight. The sudden realization and acceptance of how things really are."

Daniel frowned. "What are you saying, Bill?"

"That maybe Lydia, as we knew her, really is gone, and we need to stop looking for her to come back to us."

Daniel shook his head in denial.

"Think about it, Daniel. She's known us only six weeks. *Six weeks*. She's like a child who was stolen from her home in infancy and not returned until adulthood, or someone who's just moved here from out of town. We can't expect her to come back and step into the life that we all had planned for her." Tears brought a sad sparkle to the older man's eyes. "I know she's tried. She's given her best shot at giving us back what we lost, but for whose sake? Hers or ours?"

Propping his elbow on the chair arm, Daniel massaged his throbbing temple. He didn't want to accept what Bill was saying. Didn't want to accept that Lydia was really gone. Even though, deep down, he suspected he had known it for some time. "So what are you saying?" he repeated. "That we should just forget about the past? Pretend it never happened?"

Bill gave his head a solemn shake. "I don't think any of us could do that, or that anyone, including *Sara,* would expect us to. I'm just saying that maybe it's time we stopped trying to hold onto it, and accept the gift that we've been given in return." His gaze bore into Daniel's for a wise and perceptive moment. "A good place to start would be by letting go of all that guilt you've been toting around for the last five years."

Daniel shifted his gaze to the cold, empty fireplace. He still found it amazing that Bill Quinn had never blamed him for his daughter's disappearance, for not taking that trip with her.

"Fate dealt us all a bitter blow that night, Daniel," Bill continued. "There wasn't one of us who didn't stop and ask ourselves if there was something we could have done." Voice mellowing, he added, "No one blames you, Son. Don't you think it's time you stopped blaming yourself?"

Daniel continued to massage his temple, continued staring unseeingly at the fireplace. He didn't know how to respond to all that Bill had said. Daniel needed time to think, weigh everything out, and to pray.

As though sensing Daniel's need for solitude, Bill stood. Daniel started to follow suit, but the older man stopped him with an understanding hand on his shoulder. "Don't get up. I'll see myself out."

Daniel nodded and settled back in his chair. Would he ever muddle through all the confusion? With a sigh, he raised his hand and started kneading his temple again. Was anything in life ever certain? At the moment, he could think of only one thing.

"Bill?" Daniel called just before the man exited from the room.

In the open doorway, Bill turned back.

"This whole Lydia being Sara thing may still have me a bit addled," Daniel said. "But there is one thing I'm not confused about. I love your daughter. Of that, I'm certain."

A knowing gleam warmed the older man's eyes. "I know you do, Daniel. If I didn't, I wouldn't be here."

Bill started through the door again, then apparently struck by another thought, he stopped and turned around. "One more thing. You told Jen that your love for Lydia hasn't changed. Are you sure about that?"

"If anything, I love her more."

"More? Or different?"

Both came to mind so quickly that Daniel blinked in surprise. He did love her more, stronger, deeper than before. And that love was different, because *she* was different.

Daniel gave the man standing at the doorway a blank look of dawning enlightenment. Why, he'd gone and fallen in love all over again, with a woman named Sara.

Bill simply smiled. "That's what I thought. Now, all you have to do is convince my daughter."

ᴥ

Dear Diary

Sara pulled her hand away from her new journal and studied the words she'd just written. For some reason, they didn't feel right. She drew in a deep breath and released it through pursed lips. Why did she feel a need to start a journal anyway? What benefit was there in telling your innermost secrets to a book?

"Mama, can me an' Mittens go climb on the rocks?"

Holding a strand of windblown hair away from her face, Sara looked up at the child standing beside her in a neon pink bathing suit. A gray ball of fur swarmed around her ankles, sniffing at a bottle of sunscreen lying on the beach blanket where Sara sat. For some reason known only to a child's mind, Chloe was fascinated with the mountain of huge rocks that was an extension of the jetty at the end of the island.

"No, you may not," Sara answered, adjusting the strap that had slid off her daughter's shoulder. "You might fall and get hurt or slip and get your foot trapped between the rocks." She pushed Chloe's sunglasses up her nose. "Besides, the tide's coming in and you might get washed away. Then what would I do without my little girl?"

"You'd cry and cry, just like you do for Daniel."

Sara blinked back the stinging onslaught of tears. Why did the child have to be so perceptive?

Chloe tilted her head, the end of her ponytail brushing one shoulder. "Is he ever coming back to see us?"

Chloe had questioned Daniel's absence several times over the past four days, but Sara didn't have the strength yet to explain to her child that he would no longer be a constant part of their lives. She wanted to wait until she got past the stage of sporadic weeping that often hit her unawares at any given time of the day. "Honey, Daniel is your very good friend, and he loves you very much. I'm sure he'll find a way to see you soon."

"But don't he want to be your friend anymore?"

Probably not. But she couldn't tell Chloe that. "Daniel is everybody's friend," she said, hoping the answer would satisfy her daughter. Before the child could come up with a response, Sara added, "Now, you and Mittens go on and finish your sand castle. We only have a few more minutes before we have to go in."

Chloe and Mittens scampered a few feet away to a lumpy mound of sand that looked more like a range of bald mountains than a castle. The calming call of a seagull harmonized with the voice of the waves crashing against the jetty. While Sara listened to the beauty of the sea song, she watched her daughter and reminded herself that she was a woman truly blessed. She had a God who would never forsake her. A child who was healthy and happy. A family who loved her and—although they were still a bit taken aback—supported her desire to legally change her name to Sara Lydia Quinn. Oh, yes, and she had Mittens. The cat had promptly become a comforting, permanent member of hers and Chloe's family.

The only thing missing was Daniel.

She forced a breath past the catch in her throat. *Four out of five isn't bad,* she reminded herself. One couldn't have it all.

With a fingertip, she caught a tear trying to escape the corner of her eye. " 'For I know the thoughts that I think toward you, saith the LORD,' " she whispered to herself, " 'thoughts of peace, and not of evil, to give you an expected end.' "

The verse had given her a sense of peace in the midst of every storm she had ridden over the past five years, and it gave peace now. She had to be thankful she'd found out Daniel's true feelings for her before one day he woke up next to her and realize he'd married a stranger.

But peace did not take away the pain. At least, not yet anyway. She pressed a palm against the weight on her chest. Even when her heart was once again able to reach beyond pain to sweet remembrance, things would never be the same. There would never be another Daniel.

She turned her attention back to the book and poised her pen over the paper. *Dear Diary,* she read, then realized what was wrong. With one quick stoke, she marked through *Dear Diary* and wrote *Dear God.*

This would be her prayer journal. The place she went to daily to talk to God and thank Him for all the goodness and blessings He had brought to her life, a place to pray for others and ask for strength. Especially in the days of loneliness ahead.

She wrote nonstop for ten minutes, finishing her first entry with:

> *God, please help Daniel understand why I had to let him go. Help him get through the pain, for I know, right now, he is hurting. He's lost so much. Help him find the woman who is right for him. I know there's one out there somewhere. Someone who will make him happy. Someone as true and kind and as generous as he. He has too much love to offer not to share his life with someone like that. And I promise, when that time comes, I will be happy for him.*
>
> *Love,*
> *Sara*

She blotted the teardrops from the page with the end of a beach towel and closed the journal. Then she wiped the moisture from her face with her hands. She'd get through this. Somehow, by the grace of God, she would survive.

She glanced up to check on Chloe. Her bucket lay overturned in the midst of the lumpy sand castle, and her blue shovel was stuck up in the sand. But Chloe and Mittens were gone.

"Chloe?" Her pulse quickened as she searched the shrinking beach, then surged with alarm when she located her daughter trying to climb up the jetty rocks. "Chloe!" She threw the book aside and vaulted up in a run. "Chloe! Wait!"

Thank God, Chloe complied.

Sara ran out into knee-deep water and scooped up her daughter off the rocks. She trudged back to dry land and set the child down on solid ground. Then, kneeling, she clasped Chloe's upper arms. "Chloe, what has gotten into you?" The child rarely disobeyed a request. "I told you not to climb on the rocks. You could get hurt!"

Sunglasses now gone, Chloe looked up at her mother

through worried blue eyes. Her small chin quivered. "But I have to get Mittens. She's gone after the fish."

"What fish?"

Chloe pointed toward the water. Sara's line of vision followed her daughter's pointing finger, and sure enough, there was Mittens halfway out the jetty, slapping at small fish jumping out of the swirling waves. *"Mittens,"* Sara chided under her breath. Didn't the crazy cat realize her legs were three inches—not three feet—long?

"We have to get her, Mommy," came Chloe's small, panic-stricken voice. "Or she'll wash away."

Sara turned back to her daughter. "Okay, Chloe. I want you to go sit on the steps and don't move. No matter what."

"What are you going to do?"

"I'm going after Mittens."

"But what if you get washed away?"

"I won't," she said, hoping she was right. "I'll be very careful. But, if something does happen, and I can't get back, then you go to the house and call 9-1-1. Okay?"

"Okay."

"Now, go sit down, and stay there until I get back."

With bare feet, Sara gingerly negotiated the jagged rocks until the wind caught her off guard, making her lose her footing and scrape an ankle. She picked her way over the rest of the rubble on hands and knees, clenching her teeth a little harder every time Mittens ignored her summons.

"I'm going to wring your skinny little neck when I get you back to shore," she ground out as she crawled up onto the six-inch wide jetty platform. Her hand slipped and snagged a small splinter. Wiping the blood that seeped from her palm on the seat of her cutoffs, she added, "If you don't make me shark bait first."

❧

Cradling a small bouquet of mixed flowers in one arm, Daniel climbed the front steps of the cottage. He had no idea what he was going to say to her when she opened the door—and she would open it, even if he had to use his key first. He just knew that somehow he had to convince her he loved the woman she was now—not the woman she used to be. That was a love whose time was past. Like Bill had said, it was time to let it go. Accept what God had given him in return—and Daniel was wholeheartedly ready to do that. Now, if he could only persuade her to accept him.

He stepped up to the door, his stomach a knot of nerves and anticipation. He'd do whatever it took to plead his case. After all, it was a matter of life and death. *His*.

With a deep, bracing breath, he rang the doorbell. What should he say to get her to hear him out before slamming the door in his face? Maybe he could start with something like, *Hi. My name is Daniel. What's yours?*

Almost immediately, he shook his head. Too corny sounding. And she'd probably never fall for it, anyway. He glanced down at the flowers resting in the crook of his arm. He had chosen a mixture of painted daisies, sweet-smelling lavender, morning glories, and several other species he couldn't name, all nestled in a bed of pink baby's breath. They reminded him of a field of wildflowers, and he had known the minute he saw them in the florist's window that Sara would love them, a lot more than she would a box of long-stem roses.

He looked back at the door. Where was she? He'd expected to hear some activity from her or Chloe by now. He knew they were home; her car was in the garage area beneath the house.

He rang the doorbell again, waited about half-a-minute, then bounded down the steps and headed for the narrow path carved through the thick island flora that led to the back of the house. Maybe she and Chloe were on the beach, which would be even better. That way, she couldn't slam the door in his face.

When he broke through the thick cloud of plant life, he scanned the beach area. He found only an abandoned beach blanket and sand bucket. One corner of his mouth tipped. She and Chloe were probably exploring. His gaze drifted a little farther down the beach to the jetty, and his steps faltered. Sara was crawling out on the narrow platform, about to be swallowed up by the roiling waves of the incoming high tide.

Terror slammed into him at the same time adrenaline kicked in, and he didn't stop to think. Taking off in a dead run, he screamed, "Saaaaraaaa!"

୬

The waves slapped at Sara's hands and knees, but she was almost there. Only a couple more feet and she would have Mittens, who had realized the error of her ways and had climbed up onto the top of one of the poles anchoring the jetty.

Sara paused, listening. Had someone called her name? Her instant of distraction left her unprepared for the next wave that sloshed over the jetty, and her left knee slipped off the platform. A jolt of alarm quickened her pulse and she steadied herself. Best keep her mind on what she was doing.

She hooked her hand around the quivering cat; as she pulled the kitten to her chest, she hesitated again. Someone had called her name, and it sounded like Daniel.

Twisting her head around, she found him sprinting down the beach toward her, waving his arms over his head and yelling, "Sara! Wait! I'm coming!"

Something cold and powerful hit her on her blind side, and the next thing she knew, she was being swallowed by the churning dark waters of the Atlantic.

୬

"Sara? Sara? Can you hear me?"

There it was again. Daniel calling her name. Calling her up out of the darkness. She must be dreaming.

Something cold and wet covered her mouth and forced air into her lungs. Her body convulsed. She coughed as air rushed from her chest, then her body settled back down.

"That's it, baby," came that beautiful voice again. "Come on back to me."

Slowly, she opened her eyes, and there he was, kneeling over her, nursing the back of her head with one hand, his wet hair dripping on her face. Oh, but he was beautiful.

"Oh, thank God." He buried his face against her shoulder. "Thank God, you're alive. I thought I had lost you."

Instinctively, she raised her hand to the back of his head and held it there. As the fog evaporated from her mind, she struggled to sit up. "Chloe?"

He drew back, cradling her face with his palm. "She's fine. She's sitting on the steps with one of the neighbors."

"Mittens?"

"She's fine, too. You were still holding onto her when I got to you."

Assured her family was safe, she reached up and laid her hand against his cool, damp cheek. "Sara." It wasn't a question, but a statement of awe and wonder.

His eyes crinkled. "Yes, sweetheart. You're fine, too."

"No, you. You called me 'Sara.' When I was out on the jetty, and you were running toward me, without stopping or thinking or. . .anything, you called me Sara."

His brow furrowed in thought, then smoothed. "Yes, I guess I did."

The center of her being flooded with joy that extended to every fiber in her body. "Thank you, Daniel. You saved my life today, in more ways than one."

☙

"We're going to keep you overnight, just for observation."

Sara let her head flop back on the pillow. "Is that really necessary, Dr. Bayne?"

He shifted his gaze from the chart he was writing, peering at her over his reading glasses. "Probably not, but I'd rather be safe—"

"I know. I know. You'd rather be safe than sorry."

"That's right." He patted her knee. "Now, there are some very anxious people outside waiting to see you. I think I'd better let them in before they knock down the door."

Her father and Chloe came in first. After greeting them both with a hug and kiss, she settled Chloe on the bed next to her. "Where are the others?" she asked her father.

"They're outside. The doctor said we could come in only two at a time. Hospital rules." He eased himself down on the edge of the bed and picked up her hand. "Jen and Margaret will come in next, then your mother and I will take Chloe home with us for the night. Since Daniel's going to stay the night, he decided he'd take his turn last."

Her eyes widened. "Daniel's spending the night?"

Her father sent her a teasing wink. "I gave my permission, as long as he keeps himself in the guest cot."

A bit discomfited, she ducked her head. He lifted it back up with a finger beneath her chin. "I don't think we could run him out of this place tonight with a shotgun. That young man loves you, Sara. *You.* I hope you've figured that out by now."

"I have, Dad. And I love him, too."

"An' me, too," Chloe chimed in, and a round of laughter followed.

Her mother and Jennifer kept their visit short, then Mr. and Mrs. Matthews stuck their heads in to express their happiness that she'd survived her cat-rescuing venture unharmed.

The second Daniel's parent's left, Sara adjusted the pillows supporting her back and combed her fingers through her tangled hair. She'd give a week's wages for a mirror and brush right now. She had to be a mess. Wetting her lips, she straightened her covers and clasped her hands in her lap. She hadn't been this nervous the first time she had met Daniel, six weeks ago in Chicago.

He hesitated in the doorway, a dream in the shadows, then strolled into the glow of the overhead lights, her knight who had come to carry her away to happily ever after. A leather overnight bag dangled from one hand. Someone, his parents probably, had apparently brought him some fresh clothes, but he hadn't taken the time to change yet. His navy slacks and yellow pullover shirt were both pretty much a mess, and he hadn't even combed his hair. But he was the most beautiful sight she had ever seen.

He stopped a few feet inside the door and tossed the overnight bag to a nearby chair. "Hi," he said, dazzling her with a sheepish grin.

If she didn't know better, she'd say he sounded shy. "Hi, yourself."

"My name's Daniel. What's yours?"

A silent message passed between them. The promise of a new beginning was sealed. Anticipation and excitement danced across her skin. "Sara. My name is Sara."

"Sara," he mused, as though testing the flavor of the word on his tongue. Slowly and deliberately, he ambled forward. "I like that name," he added as though he approved of the taste.

The fluttering butterflies in her stomach veered off course, darting around in a dozen different directions, bumping into each other. "Thanks. Daniel's nice, too."

"You think so?"

"Yeah. I think so."

He eased down on the edge of the bed, captured her hands in his. His tender gaze consumed her. "So, Sara. What are you doing tonight? And tomorrow night? And for the rest of your life?"

She shrugged a shoulder. "I dunno. Wanna get married?" It was bold, it was forward, and it was cheeky. But it was right. She *knew* it was right.

A spark of surprise and delight widened his eyes. Then, almost as quickly as his elation had come, it faded. He released one of her hands and pressed his forefinger to her lips. "Hold that thought."

She kissed his fingertip. "Got it."

Just before he dropped his gaze, she caught a glimpse of pain. A pain, she sensed, he had carried too long. She wanted to lift her arms and embrace him, comfort him. But something told her to wait. To let him explain.

He recaptured both of her hands, caressing the backs of her fingers with his thumbs. "There's something I need to tell you about the trip to New York."

"Okay."

Lifting his lids, he met her unwavering gaze. He could live an eternity drowning in those eyes, eyes that showered him with love and devotion. A quick wave of apprehension clenched his stomach. After he told her why she took that New York trip alone, would she still look at him like he hung the moon?

He wasn't sure he wanted to find out, but he knew she deserved to know the truth. "I was supposed to go with you on that trip, Sara. I had my room reservations made and my bags packed, but I backed out at the last minute because a court case got pushed up a week on the trial schedule."

She waited a moment, as though she expected him to say more. When he didn't right away, she gave a nonchalant shrug. "So? You're an attorney, Daniel. I was a dress shop owner. We were both doing our jobs."

"Yes, but I could have let my dad handle the case. I could have talked to the judge, told him I couldn't change my plans. I could have done a number of things, but I didn't." Shame pressed down upon him, almost choking him. "I chose my work over you, Sara, and because I did, you suffered a brutal attack and lost your memory. Can you ever forgive me for that?"

"There's nothing to forgive, Daniel," she said without hesitation.

Her lack of pause told him she meant it. She did not blame him for her abduction. But that didn't change the fact that it had happened, that because of his self-serving attitude, she had been alone that night.

"Daniel, do you ever ask yourself 'What if?' " she added

after a prolonged moment of silence.

He studied her face, the wisdom in her expression, and found there a deep well of understanding. "Yes," he admitted. "All the time."

"I've done that a lot myself over the past six weeks. What if I hadn't taken that exit? What if I had stayed on the interstate? What if I had been a few minutes earlier and been involved in the accident that caused the traffic delay?" She pulled her hands free of his and framed her face with his palms. "What if you *had* been with me that night, and you too had fallen prey to the men who attacked me?" Her features softened. Her eyes grew misty. "If that had happened, I suppose I would have a pretty tough time forgiving myself, too."

He shook his head. "But it wouldn't have been your fault."

"Exactly."

She gave him a moment to consider her words. "Oh, Daniel, you're such a wonderful protector. You take such good care of me and Chloe, and I know you took good care of Lydia, too. That's one of the reasons you're finding it so hard to forgive yourself.

"But it wasn't your fault. God was in control of our lives, and *no one* is to blame. And no one is holding you accountable except yourself." He felt her fingers spread over his head, as though she were trying to encompass his mind with assurance. "Let it go, Daniel. I know for an honorable heart like yours, that's easier said than done. But you can do it. With God's help, you can do anything."

Daniel knew he was looking into the face of a woman who knew what she was talking about. A woman who had awakened one day wounded, pregnant, and alone. A woman who hadn't known who she was or where she came from. A woman who had crawled up from the pits of hell and learned to stand on her own.

A woman who had taught him how to give freely and love without condition.

Looking deep into her eyes at that moment, he knew nothing from the past would ever come between them. A shadow receded from his heart, and a burden he had carried for five long years grew lighter. She was right. With God's help and her love, he could do anything. Even, one day, forgive himself.

He felt a touch of God's grace flow through him, and a surge of love flooded his soul as the last chain of bondage fell from his heart. He shifted his head and kissed her palm. "You're something else. You know that?"

"I know," she said without a single shred of vanity. Then, with a minxish grin, she grasped the front of his shirt and pulled him forward. "Now, there's this matter of a thought. . ."

He stopped with his mouth less than a breath away from hers. "Oh, yeah, as I was saying. What are you doing tonight?" He brushed her lips with his. "And tomorrow night?" He brushed her lips again. "And for the rest of your life?"

"I dunno. Wanna get married?"

"Yes, Sara. Yes, I do."

The silence that followed was filled with faith, hope, and love. All three. But the greatest of these was love.

And in the midst of that love was forgiveness.

A Letter To Our Readers

Dear Reader:

In order that we might better contribute to your reading enjoyment, we would appreciate your taking a few minutes to respond to the following questions. We welcome your comments and read each form and letter we receive. When completed, please return to the following:

Rebecca Germany, Fiction Editor
Heartsong Presents
PO Box 719
Uhrichsville, Ohio 44683

1. Did you enjoy reading *Familiar Strangers?*
    ☐ Very much. I would like to see more books
    by this author!
    ☐ Moderately
    I would have enjoyed it more if _____

    _____

    _____

2. Are you a member of **Heartsong Presents**? Yes ☐ No ☐
    If no, where did you purchase this book?_____

    _____

3. How would you rate, on a scale from 1 (poor) to 5 (superior), the cover design?_____

4. On a scale from 1 (poor) to 10 (superior), please rate the following elements.

    _____ Heroine   _____ Plot

    _____ Hero   _____ Inspirational theme

    _____ Setting   _____ Secondary characters

5. These characters were special because_____

_____

_____

6. How has this book inspired your life?_____

_____

_____

7. What settings would you like to see covered in future
    Heartsong Presents books?_____

_____

_____

8. What are some inspirational themes you would like to see
    treated in future books?_____

_____

_____

9. Would you be interested in reading other **Heartsong
    Presents** titles?   Yes ☐   No ☐

10. Please check your age range:
    ☐ Under 18   ☐ 18-24   ☐ 25-34
    ☐ 35-45   ☐ 46-55   ☐ Over 55

11. How many hours per week do you read?_____

Name _____

Occupation _____

Address _____

City _____ State _____ Zip _____

Reunions

The spark of love stands the test of
time and is fanned
to a flame as four
couples are reunited.
These contemporary
novellas include
four reunion
celebrations—high
school, college,
family, and organ
donors—that will
tug at the tightest of heartstrings.
paperback, 352 pages, 5 ⁹⁄₁₆" x 8"

❤ ❤ ❤ ❤ ❤ ❤ ❤ ❤ ❤ ❤ ❤ ❤ ❤ ❤ ❤ ❤ ❤

❤ ❤ ❤ ❤ ❤ ❤ ❤ ❤ ❤ ❤ ❤ ❤ ❤ ❤ ❤ ❤

····Hearts♥ng····

Any 12 Heartsong Presents titles for only $26.95 *

HEARTSONG PRESENTS *TITLES AVAILABLE NOW:*

(If ordering from this page, please remember to include it with the order form.)

Presents